Mating Scent

Morgan Clan Bears
Book 4

THERESA HISSONG

Disclaimer:
This book is a work of fiction. Any resemblance to any person, living or dead is purely coincidental. The names of people, places, and/or things are all created from the author's mind and are only used for entertainment.

Due to the content, this book is recommended for adults 18 years and older.

©2022Theresa Hissong
All Rights Reserved

Cover Design:
Gray Publishing Services

Editing by:
Heidi Ryan
Amour the Line Editing

Formatting By:
Imagine Ink Designs

Follow Theresa at
Authortheresahissong.com
Or
www.facebook.com/authortheresahissong

Dedication:

To you, the reader…I thank you for sticking with my bears through all of their stories. These bears will always hold a special place in my heart, and I hope they left a mark on yours.

Table of Contents

Chapter 1..1
Chapter 2..11
Chapter 3..19
Chapter 4..25
Chapter 5..41
Chapter 6..59
Chapter 7..71
Chapter 8..79
Chapter 9..97
Chapter 10..105
Chapter 11..121
Chapter 12..127
Chapter 13..139
Chapter 14..151
Chapter 15..167
Epilogue..173

Chapter 1

*L*uca added logs to the fire and poured himself another glass of whiskey. It was late, but he wasn't in the mood for sleep. He hadn't slept well for the past two years since his brother, Ransom, was killed at the hands of humans.

The memories flipped through his mind like the pages of a photobook; moments of time forever etched into every corner of his brain. The voices of his clan, and the voice of the panther's healer as he delivered the news to his family.

"The injury was too much for his bear to heal."

"Again, I'm sorry."

Anna Claire's screams and tears...her gut-wrenching cries.

"Fuck, damn it, stop thinking about it!" he snarled into the empty cabin.

One moment, the whiskey glass was in his hand, and the next, it was shattered against the fireplace, fueling the flames of the fire.

He wasn't okay, and his clan knew it. The Morgan brothers, Drake, Rex, and Gunnar, were always with him, working with him. They kept him busy, and rightly so. He respected the hell out of them, and he wouldn't have been safe if he'd stayed in his uncle's clan. If it wasn't for his cousin, Anna Claire, he would probably be dead like his brother.

That was the crux of the whole fucking thing. If they'd stayed, and his old clan had not been killed, he and his brother, Ransom, would've died anyway. But the humans came, after they'd found safety, and taken his only brother…his best friend, from him anyway.

That would fuck up anyone.

A glance at the clock proved he really needed to sleep, because it was time for spring planting and he was on duty in less than five hours. He set his alarm on his phone and fell into the recliner, jumping right back up when the alarm sounded.

"Damn it," he cursed, groaning as he stood. He stunk of cheap whiskey and two days of no showering. It didn't take long to run the soap over his body, shampoo in his hair, and a good two minutes of hot water to get his blood flowing.

It didn't help his fucking bear was starting to stir. They'd only been out of hibernation for three weeks, but his nature didn't care. It was mating season, and he'd go

Mating Scent

another year without finding a mate.

It was probably for the best because he was in no shape to care for a female. He couldn't even take care of himself.

After he showered, leaving his long, black hair to dry naturally, he grabbed a travel mug of coffee and left his cabin. The elders were still inside, and he was okay that he didn't have to converse with them at six in the morning. He'd try to check on them after he finished work, though. It was the only routine he'd adopted since he'd been on his own for the last two years.

Rex was walking from the main house as he arrived at the barn, meeting Luca at the doors.

"Morning," Rex grumbled. It wasn't like the middle brother to be so grumpy, but it didn't take long for him to realize why. It only took one scent that lingered on his skin to answer the question.

"Ada is with young?" Luca boasted, slapping Rex on the back. Gods, it was refreshing to have a bit of good news for once. "If you'd like to stay with your mate today, I can work alone, you know."

The last thing a male would ever do is take his friend away from a newly pregnant mate. Even with his own problems, Luca knew Rex's connection to Ada was more important. It was ingrained in the males to be protective no matter their own problems. A male bear's heart and soul belonged to their mate.

"Actually," Rex paused, narrowing his eyes, "I think we need to work together today. We haven't seen you in a few days."

"Before you ask, I'm sober," Luca grumbled.

"I know, but I can still smell last night's whiskey over the soap you used in the shower this morning," Rex scolded. "Man, we know how bad you hurt. We all do, but it's been…"

"Two fucking years!" Luca lashed out. "I know how long it's been…to the fucking day since the humans took my brother from me, Rex."

Luca pushed at his beast, knowing full well it was on edge, too. And the last thing he needed was for his bear to shift. The Morgan Clan was all he had, and he couldn't go on without them. He doubted he'd be kicked out, because Anna Claire would fight for him. However, it wasn't always guaranteed to have a home anywhere in the world. He'd learned that the hard way.

He hadn't been wanted by his own father, and just like Anna Claire's mother, his and Ransom's mother had suspiciously died when they were barely teenagers. He didn't even have to investigate it, because he knew his clan had had something to do with it. They left the elders alive, and he never understood why…neither did the others.

"We have work to do, Rex. I'm sorry," Luca sighed. "It's mating season, and my bear is on edge. I just want to work to keep my mind off of everything."

Rex watched him with a concerned look for several seconds before he nodded and grabbed a cooler from the work table. "Let's get to the fields, but first…I'd like to run over to Gaia's for breakfast. How does that sound?"

"I could use a good meal," Luca agreed as his anger deflated. Food sounded amazing. He'd just woken from

Mating Scent

his hibernation, and he still hadn't eaten enough to account for the time he'd spent drunk or asleep during the past winter.

Mara rushed around the diner, refilling coffee cups as fast as she could. It was a Monday, and from the looks of it, most of the town was skipping work for an early morning breakfast. Most of the men in the room were farmers, and she giggled to herself. They were ready to work, but not quite yet. Spring had arrived, and it was the first decently warm day they'd had since the fall, and the sun was shining bright.

Mara had been at the diner long enough to notice when the Morgan family came in and spoke to her boss in private. She knew they were a clan of bears, but Gaia didn't scent of a shifter. She tried to keep her own hearing down so she didn't pry when they would slip off to her boss's office.

The bear clan had been through some type of tragedy two years prior. One of the unmated bears was killed, but Mara didn't know how or why. She'd accidentally heard them talking about it one afternoon. When she'd realized what she was hearing wasn't for her expert ears, she left the storage room next to Gaia's office as quick as she could before anyone could suspect her of eavesdropping.

Two years…whew. It was crazy how your life could change in such a short time. Back then, she was on the run from her old coven, but she'd taken care of her old life so it couldn't come back to haunt her. The world didn't know about her, nor did she care for them to, either.

Mara was working on her own demons, and she'd finally found a place to call home where she could hide from those who would wish her harm.

But she wasn't hiding a shifter secret. No, her kind was a curse…a design flaw. An evil demon turned her into the one thing she'd only seen in movies as a young female.

A vampire.

Mara didn't crave human blood, and she was nothing like what the movies portrayed a vampire to be for entertainment. No, she was built to feed off of shifters, and she hated herself for it. Thankfully, she could still survive on human food, but it didn't keep her strong enough. As it was, she hadn't fully fed in over two years, leaving her twenty pounds lighter. She was starving.

There were no bear shifters around to give her their blood. There had been a clan that could've been a good source for her, but they'd all been killed by the Morgan Clan a while back. She didn't know what exactly had transpired, but like the news she'd overheard about Ransom, the murder of the evil bear clan didn't shock her as much as it should. If a bear clan dealt out shifter justice to another clan who was doing inhumane things to their people, she understood why they'd done what they had. She would've done the same thing.

With the lack of blood, her body had shrunken…her muscles disappearing, because without that blood, she was nothing more than a human with some really sharp teeth. Funny how the gods liked to play with their creations, huh?

Fuck them.

Mara rolled her eyes and grabbed plates of food to feed the farmers, but when she turned, the front door opened. Her mouth watered and her fangs tried to thicken at the scent of an unmated bear entering the diner.

"Hey, Mara," Gaia called out. "Everything okay?"

"Oh, no, I'm fine…it's fine," she said, jutting her chin toward the door. "Your friends are here."

It was bullshit that she could only drink from bears, and really fucked up that she was made to be that way. Why bears? Why not any shifter? Her only training at the change was to stay away from any shifters who had to have alphas to keep them alive, and as far as she knew, bears were her only option.

Her coven lived with a clan who'd offered their blood for the vampire's protection. The first several years, she'd been brainwashed into trading her body for the unmated male's blood. She wasn't a whore, but her guilt over what she was forced to do was just too much, and she'd packed her things in the night and left.

Eventually, she ended up back with the male who'd turned her because she was desperate for blood. After a while, he'd begun forcing her to have sex with some of the bears to keep the pact between them when the bears grew tired of the vampires and their reign over the clan. When Mara was caught trying to leave again, she was attacked by her maker. She was older and wiser by then, and she used her anger to drive a wooden stake through his heart after she'd regained her full strength.

Since then, she'd suppressed her need for their blood and accepted that she wouldn't be strong anymore. In fact, ignoring your need for blood did not kill you as a vampire. No, it basically made you a human again. A human with a terrible craving for blood.

Her only source of blood was from random deliveries once a month from a no-named male she'd connected with online. Four pints a month…that was it. That was all she needed to at least have the energy to get up in the morning and go to work.

If she ever fed on a shifter again, it would turn her into something stronger than them…stronger than anything out there. She'd have her full abilities back…her senses…her immortality. But it would take a lot of blood to do that.

A lot more than a pint a week.

But there was a cost…there was *always* a cost. Someone would get hurt, and she'd done enough of that over the years.

For that reason, she had moved to this small town just south of Memphis, Tennessee, hoping to get away from the vile shifters she'd crossed in the other towns and cities she'd lived in since being turned. It was better for her mental health to stay out of the big cities anyway. She needed peace and quiet away from a lot of shifters, but it turned out she'd moved to a town rich with them.

Thankfully, most of the local shifters were panthers, and they had an alpha. If she'd tried to feed on a shifter with an alpha, her cover would've been blown. Leaders of shifter groups knew everything about their members.

Mating Scent

Mara wanted to stay hidden.

What she really needed to do was get the hell out of the south and move north…maybe to Canada. She might find a clan up there she could work for and possibly meet a male of worth who would sweep her off her feet and accept her for who she really was when his bear recognized her as his mate after they came out of winter hibernation in the spring.

"Mara," Gaia called out. "Can you take Rex and Luca some coffee? I'm swamped. Get their food order while you're at it."

"Sure thing," she replied and grabbed her notepad. The closer she got to the table, the stronger the male's scent became. She'd seen him before, but she'd never noticed much about him other than his long hair and sour attitude.

Canada was looking better and better each day.

"Good morning," she greeted with a smile, but without showing her teeth. They were aching. "Gaia wanted me to get your orders and start you off with some coffee. She's a little busy at the moment."

"That's fine," Rex Morgan said, waving off any concern. "We are starving, and maybe putting off work for an extra hour this morning." She laughed at his teasing, and he followed, but the other male, Luca, just stared at his menu.

"What can I get for you?" she pressed, hoping the male would look up.

Rex rambled off his large order, and she turned toward Luca. When he didn't move, she frowned. "Luca? Can I get you some food?"

The moment his head turned slowly toward her, she scented him again. It was spring for the bears, and the mating scent coming off of his body had her taking a step back. It was strong…like the most expensive cologne mixed with the scents of the earth.

"Luca?" Rex growled, kicking his friend under the table.

Luca shook his head and gathered himself. She saw his brown eyes, but not before the specks of gold were completely gone. His bear was present.

"What's your name?" he whispered just low enough that only she could hear.

"Mara," she blurted, pressing her lips together. He should've already known her name, because he'd been coming to the diner since she started there two years ago. "It's Mara."

Chapter 2

Gaia was in her office, brewing up a sunny day for the farmers, but once Luca entered the diner with Rex Morgan, she felt the earth shift.

Mara.

Mating Season.

And with that came a whole host of problems. She'd hired the female, knowing she was a vampire, but a vampire who was broken and scared. The last two years had helped, though. She was stronger in mind, but not in body.

Gaia knew the fucking gods had played a part in working with demons to make the vampires, forcing some of them to only feed on the shifters.

Her shifters.

The bears.

There was something different about Mara, though, and while she'd not seen Luca much since his brother had been killed two years ago, she had never thought that the vampire waitress was going to be his mate.

What worried her was if Luca could actually handle this year's mating season, or if he and Mara were to connect. The moment he walked in the door, she knew it was out of her hands. It didn't matter about the gods, demons, or her being Mother Earth...when a mate connection was happening, there was nothing she could do to stop it.

The only saving grace she had was that Luca needed help, and so did Mara. Maybe, just maybe, this was going to be a good thing.

She'd told Mara she was busy, and she used that as an excuse to play around with the forecast...building clouds in the western sky.

The moment she entered the diner, she heard the first rumble of thunder off in the distance as she watched Luca look up toward Mara to place his order. Her eyes fell on her old friend's son, Rex Morgan, and saw his eyes narrow on hers.

She gave him a little shrug, a saucy smirk, and mouthed, "*Mating Season*". To which the Morgan brother shook his head and leaned back in his seat. Today would not be a day for planting seeds.

Today was going to be the day Luca O'Kelly found someone to live for.

Mating Scent

Luca's bear was clawing at his skin to grab the female and tuck her under his arm so he could take her back to his cabin. Something changed the moment he caught her scent. She wasn't human or shifter. No, she was something else, and for some reason, it was everything his bear desired.

It took several seconds to get his eyes under control before he could turn toward her, and when he did, the scent she possessed was so much stronger. The beautiful, dark-haired female was small, and his first instinct was to protect her. His second…was to touch her…to mate her…care for her.

Their scents mingled; his mating one and the natural essence of whatever she was.

Her scent was powerful. It was like it was created for him, and he wanted it all over his skin.

But his heart sank as he mumbled out an order. He wasn't worthy of a mate. If he couldn't keep his brother alive, how could he care for a female?

His hormones overrode his guilt, and he inhaled softly as he and his bear memorized her scent. There was something about the waitress, Mara, that piqued his interest besides his need to claim her as his mate.

She was different, and surely, she wasn't human.

One more inhale, and he realized she wasn't like the men who killed his brother…nor was she like him. No, Mara was something different.

"Two big plate breakfasts and coffee?" Mara pressed as she scribbled something down on her little notepad, giving them a nod with the promise of returning shortly with their coffee.

He heard Rex agree, but he couldn't stare at the tiny female. So, he looked down at his menu as he picked it off the plastic table liner, handing it over to the Morgan brother. He didn't trust himself to do anything that would cause his hand to brush against hers. That would've been a bad idea.

As soon as the waitress walked away, a heavy hand landed on his wrist. When he looked up, Rex was staring at him with a smirk. "Find your mate?"

"She's not like us…or them," Luca mumbled, turning his head toward her as she returned to the table with their coffee. Luckily, Rex didn't respond right away.

They gave her a respectful nod as she served them, and once she left, Rex leaned closer with his eyes still brown. Thank fuck he didn't have his bear present, because it might've thrown Luca into a rage.

That woman was going to be his mate.

"That's Gaia's girl, and she's protective of Mara. So, whatever you have planned, you need to take it slow," Rex warned. "I also scent her differences, but until you know what she is, I'd be careful."

"I have nothing of worth that would persuade a female to be my mate," Luca admitted, knowing he shouldn't be airing his business out in public. "Look at me, Rex. I'm a mess. I can't even take care of myself…let alone a mate."

"That's not true," Rex sighed and leaned back into the vinyl booth seat. "I know all too well how hard it is to find yourself when you scent your mate. Your mind will try to talk you out of what is sitting right in front of you until you finally accept what your animal is telling you.

Mating Scent

It'll change you, man."

"I don't think I'm able to change yet, my friend," he said, toasting his truth by raising his coffee cup, wishing he'd brought a shot of whiskey to spike the drink.

"These things take time, believe me," Rex admitted. "We may have an animal nature, but that nature is never wrong."

"Of course, they take time," Luca said, rolling his eyes. "I doubt you touched Ada the first day you met her. Wait…scratch that. I really don't want to know the details."

"I don't want to tell you what to do, but I would at least get to know her…talk to Gaia, too," Rex suggested, but it was a statement Luca had no desire to try.

"I don't want to be the guy who tries to fill the silence by talking about nonsense with a female who can't accept me for who I've become. It's the truth, Rex. I am too far gone from mourning my brother. This mating season will not be mine."

"From the scent of it, I will have to disagree," Rex replied as he glanced at Mara, bringing their plates of food that were lined all the way up her arm.

"Let me know if you need anything else," she mentioned, but her eyes never left Luca's penetrating gaze. He couldn't figure out what she was.

"Wait," he grunted, slapping his hand on the table. "What's your name?"

"I already told you my name…it's Mara," she said with disbelief.

"No, your name…whole name," he demanded.

"Mara Wood," she blurted.

The female was just as nervous as Luca, but she never cowered from him, and that was a plus. He should've told her to run, but he didn't.

For some reason, his bear was at the surface, just under his skin, prowling…almost clawing at the need to be let out. The beast wanted to shift and show the female how big and strong he was so he could protect her from anything.

"Ms. Wood," he nodded and picked up his fork, "thank you."

The beautiful waitress scurried off, and when Luca glanced at Rex, the male had a smirk pulling at the corner of his lip. "Don't start."

"Me?" Rex chuckled. "Never."

"Bullshit," Luca mumbled as he took the first bite of food.

"Your entire demeanor changed when that female walked up to the table."

"Let's eat, Rex." Luca wasn't in the mood for talking.

The food was delicious, but it soured in his mouth the moment his mind changed and it went to his brother, Ransom. His brother would never have another meal…he would never be able to sit beside him and laugh…talk about life again.

Because he was dead.

Gone.

"Luca?"

"Luca!"

Luca shook his head and turned toward his friend. "I'm okay. I promise."

"The fuck you are," Rex growled, motioning for

Mating Scent

Mara to bring the check.

The moment she arrived, Rex asked for a box to take the food just as the rain began to pour down. "We need our check, please."

Rex was always the well-mannered one.

Luca wasn't quite sure who he was anymore.

Chapter 3

Mara rushed home after getting a message that a package had been delivered to her apartment. On the side of the box, it said, "Perishable", but it didn't say it was anything other than that.

Her mouth salivated as she used her nails to score the tape securing the box. Inside, she found several cold packs, and unfortunately only two small blood bags.

"Damn it," she cursed under her breath.

Her newest contact in Kansas City didn't send her enough to get her through the month. After two years of barely feeding on blood, she was getting too weak. Some mornings, getting out of bed was physically tiring. As she dug further into the box, there was a small note inside from Gerald.

I'm sorry, love. This was all I could spare. The clan is not as willing as they were before to accept monetary donations in exchange for their blood. I will try to access more for you next month.

Okay, two pints. She could make it work. Two pints would at least help her energy.

Right?

She placed one of the bags in the refrigerator, and the other, she cut the top off and squeezed every last drop out of it into her mouth. She didn't dare let any of it spill over her lips. She would allow that bag of blood to run through her system and save the other one for another day.

With every second that passed, she felt its effects on her. Her muscles stopped aching, and her body warmed. Her fangs ached, wanting more, and her mind wandered to the bear, Luca. Even though she was weak, she sensed something about the male that made her sad, but she already knew about that.

It was obvious he wasn't over the death of his brother.

She tried to stay out of the shifter's affairs and their fights, because it wasn't her place to help them. Mara liked to stay out of sight. It was for the best. The last thing she needed was a rival vampire coven to pass through and take notice of her. They could possibly force her to join them, and from what she knew of covens…they wouldn't take no for an answer.

There were human hunters out there, and she'd been warned about them. With that knowledge, it solidified her plans to stay hidden. She just wanted to be

Mating Scent

left alone. Hiding in that small town was perfect for her cover, and she wanted to keep it that way.

As for now, she would continue her work at the diner, and she would be cordial to those bears.

It was obvious his mating scent was active due to the spring season, and Luca was a sexy, long-haired distraction she wanted nothing to do with because they probably didn't even know that vampires existed.

Mara really hoped they didn't, either.

Mara's scent was ingrained in his human brain. Her beauty was burned into his mind's eye, too. Luca lay in bed that night, remembering how different she was. It was hard to explain exactly what her scent reminded him of...it was sweet, but there was a dangerous hint to it that fueled his beast. Dangerous wasn't exactly the word for it. Maybe, it was dangerous strength. Luca chuckled, because that little woman probably couldn't hurt a fly.

He'd noticed, before Gaia's clouds had moved in, when the morning sun had touched her hair, there were some soft red highlights weaved into the waves of what had come loose from her ponytail. There was no use in trying to erase her image from his mind, because having her beauty there helped with all of the bad left from losing his brother.

The Morgan clan was celebrating Ada's pregnancy announcement at the main house, and as much as he didn't want to be there, he decided to go. On his way home from checking the fields, he'd stopped and bought her some new tools for her home garden; one of them being a raised bed for her herbs. She had been planting them alongside other vegetables over the last few years.

This raised bed was a quick distraction for him as he bolted the legs to the main planting space, and he figured she could put it right outside the back door where she wouldn't have to go far to tend to them as her pregnancy progressed.

When he arrived at the main house, Rex lifted his head from where he was putting some type of dish in the oven. The brother gave him a nod and leveled his eyes on Ada where she was sitting there with a small glass of tea.

"Congratulations," Luca announced, trying to put on a smile for the female. "I have a present for you, but it's outside. Want me to show you now?"

"Oh, Luca!" she cheered. "You didn't have to, but I still want to see it."

Rex, her mate, laughed as they left the kitchen and headed for the back porch. The moment she laid eyes on the planter, she turned around to thank him.

"It's perfect!" Being a shifter was tough. Ada came from his clan, but she wasn't blood-related to him. Luca knew she wanted to hug him, but she used her words to show how thankful she was. If she'd touched him, it would've hurt her. He couldn't live with that, nor would he deal with the wrath of her mate.

"I thought you could use it for the herbs you grow and dry for us," he replied with a shrug.

Mating Scent

"That's a perfect idea," she giggled. "It keeps me from pulling weeds all damn day, and I don't have to bend over once the cub gets big in my belly."

"That was my thought when I saw it at the hardware store," he admitted. Seeing Ada and even Anna Claire so happy brought a tightness to his heart, but it wasn't a sad one. It was a relief that he felt something other than pain and loss. "I'm very happy you like it."

"I do, Luca," she sobered, and he knew what was coming. "Are *you* okay?"

"Today is your day, and we are going to celebrate it with an amazing dinner," he said, changing the subject. "We can talk about me at another time."

They turned to head back into the house, but Ada stopped, spinning around. "I just worry about you."

Of course, she did…just like Anna Claire worried about him.

"These things take time, and I'm working on myself," he vowed, patting his hand over his heart as a promise and a respectful gesture. She watched him for a few seconds before giving up on her worry for him, returning to the confines of the house.

Once they entered the kitchen, Gunnar was serving the food he and his brother Rex had made. He spent the night laughing and celebrating, but it was all a ruse. He was still miserable inside, but his bear was in a headspace that kept calling out for Luca to find the female, Mara.

It didn't matter how many times he pushed his bear away, the image of her bright blue eyes and dark hair flittered through his human mind.

It was after nine when everyone decided to retire for the night. The elders had left after they'd cut the cake, promising to come by to help Ada with the raised garden he'd gifted her. The brothers were anxious to get their mates back to their quarters and their cubs.

When he excused himself after helping with dishes, he walked the path leading to the tiny cabins the Morgan clan had built for him and the elders. His cabin was built for him and Ransom, but Ransom didn't live long enough for them to even add any furniture other than two temporary beds before winter came.

With the humans attacking them, their main goal had been to make a shelter dug into the ground under each cabin without disturbing the integrity of the actual home above it. Granted, the cellars below each cabin were not up to the standards of the Morgan clan's homes below their main house, but it made for a perfect hiding spot if trouble came to their lands again.

By the time he returned to his cabin, Luca shucked off his lightweight coat and then his shirt. On the counter were several bottles of hard liquor, but that night, he walked past them. He didn't drink himself to sleep.

No, he was worn out, and immediately fell into his bed and closed his eyes. He needed sleep, but with that rest came visions and dreams about the dark-haired waitress who scented of something other than shifter or human.

What the hell was she?

Chapter 4

Gaia ran tables for the lunch crowd, splitting it with Mara. She'd finally let the rain stop, and the sun was out, drying the lands for the farmers. Everything was going as usual until she sensed the moment the sheriff walked in the door.

There was a soft wind behind him, sending his angel scent her way. She shivered, but not because she was angry he was in her domain. There was a heat to her reaction, and she tried to shake it off.

There was no reason why she should be having those reactions to a male that belonged to the gods. No, it shouldn't happen. They were two different creatures, and he was here on an assignment. She was on earth because she was bored, but stayed because of her bears.

He took his usual seat at the small breakfast bar by the register and casually ran his finger down the plastic-coated menu. He didn't look up when she approached, and she noticed there was a small wrinkle between his brows. He was deep in thought.

"Coffee, sheriff?" she asked, breaking his concentration.

"If that's the strongest thing you've got." His mumbled words worried her. Did he have another vision of danger coming?

"What's wrong?" she finally asked, crossing her arms as she leaned her back against the counter by the coffee maker.

His eyes flickered toward Mara, and he started to say something, but was interrupted by a patron coming to the counter to pay his bill. As Gaia rang up the man for his meal, Mara came over and set a plate in front of the sheriff and smiled warmly.

"We made your usual," she announced and walked away.

Gaia watched Garrett from the corner of her eye as she handed the man his change. The sheriff knew something, and it didn't sit well with her.

"Do we need to go to my office after you eat?" she asked behind gritted teeth.

"Looks like your lunch crowd needs your help," Garrett said as he took a bite of his hamburger.

For the next fifteen minutes, Gaia did her job, but her mind couldn't stray from whatever the angel was there to warn her about, and from the narrowed looks he was giving Mara, she knew it had something to do with her.

"Mara, I have to speak with the sheriff," Gaia announced as she walked past her waitress. "If you get too busy, come knock on the door."

"Yes, ma'am," Mara replied.

Gaia caught Garrett's eye and jerked her head to the side, indicating she was heading to her office in the back room. The sheriff folded the napkin on his lap and laid it across the empty plate. When he stood, everyone in the room took notice.

Garrett was a large and respected male in the human world, but only Gaia and the other shifters in the area were privy to what he really was…an angel sent there to care for those panthers.

The moment he entered her office, she scented him again, and there were no words to really describe what an angel smelled like. It was sweet, calming…almost, dare she say…heavenly.

As much as she hated the gods, for some stupid reason, she trusted Garrett. He'd come through for her bears time after time when they'd been under attack, and what confused her the most was that he didn't have to do it. He did it of his own free will.

A small part of her thought he was more or less bringing his protection of the Shaw pride to the Morgan clan. That did piss her off, because she'd made a vow to their parents many moons ago to protect them. She was a bit confused, because she actually was thankful for his help.

How messed up was that?

Ugh.

The moment he closed and locked the door, she knew something bad was coming.

"Alright, sheriff, spit it out," she barked. "What's coming?"

"It's not so much of what's coming," he hedged with a heavy sigh. "I want to know why you have a vampire working for you, and I need to know if she is going to be a problem in my town and to my panthers."

"Geez, Garrett," Gaia sighed and rolled her eyes. "Mara has been here for two damn years and you are just now noticing it?" She laughed and gave him a cocky smirk.

"Gaia," he growled. His warning tone preceded his eyes flashing white for a split second.

"You really aren't doing your job as well as you think you are," she laughed, again.

"This is *not* funny, Gaia," he barked as he moved closer to her. "Have you ever met a vampire before?"

"Yeah, yeah, yeah." Gaia waved her hand as if she was dismissing him. "Mara has no clan. She doesn't want one, and she's hiding out here. I know that they feed on shifters, but so far, none of them have come forward to rat her out. However, with her small size and how weak she is some days, I have a feeling she is more human than vampire. So, you don't have to worry about your precious panthers. Mara is not a threat to them."

Mara had shown up two years ago with bruises on her body and fear in her eyes. Gaia had never asked her who had done it, and at first, she'd thought Mara was just a human female. It didn't take long to notice she was different. What Gaia thought was an abusive male was nothing like that. Mara was a rare vampire. One who fed on shifter blood and not human. The bruises were still a mystery, but Mara had become much happier in her time working at the diner. She made enough in tips to rent a tiny home just off the old highway a few minutes away from where Gaia lived.

She came to work, and she didn't cause problems. That was all that mattered to Gaia in the beginning, but now, she felt a connection to her and considered her family.

"Has she told you what she is?" he pressed.

"Nope," Gaia said with a pop of her lip. "And I haven't asked her. It's none of my business."

"The hell it isn't," Garrett replied, stepping into her personal space. "You could be in danger."

He was doing it again, flirting with his human body, trying to dominate her. She knew him better than he realized.

"Garrett," she warned, shaking a finger at his handsome face. "Don't come in here and bully me into not helping someone in need."

His large hands wrapped around her shoulders as her back met the door. For a moment, she thought he was going to actually kiss her when his mouth moved closer to hers. Instead of the kiss, he shifted his head just the slightest, leaning toward her ear, but not before his lips grazed her cheek, sending flaming heat across the area he'd touched.

"This is my town, my business," he whispered into her ear. "If I find any dead shifters with bite marks on their throats, I will bring hell with me to take Mara from you."

With a gasp from her, he disappeared into thin air, leaving Gaia there with a racing heart and a memory of what his lips felt like across her skin. Her eyes swirled at the thought of that man coming for Mara.

How could she hate him for threatening Mara, but still respect him for his help with her bears at the same time?

Luca finished his work for the day, proud of himself for getting one of the fields planted. He'd been up since dawn, and the sun was just starting to sink below the horizon. He locked everything up and decided to stop by the panther's bar, The Deuce, to have a beer by himself. He wasn't ready to return to the cabin he'd hand-built with his brother. It was just too quiet without Ransom there.

His mind was always at war with itself. One moment, he would be fine…the next, he would go back into mourning like it'd just happened. Then there was mating season, and with it, he found a female that sparked his bear's interest. He'd be lying if he said Mara Wood didn't do something to his human half either.

He parked his truck at the end of the building, and for a Tuesday night, it was a little busy. The moment he walked in, the jukebox was playing a song he'd liked since he was a young boy. With his parents already deceased, the song meant a lot to him. He listened to it

Mating Scent

often.

Over the scent of hamburgers, chicken, and bottles of beer, he caught her unique scent. He hadn't seen Mara since the morning before, and his eyes quickly searched the area to find her. She was alone at one of the small booths in the back by the pool tables. The panthers who worked there gave him a respectful nod as he went to her. He didn't wait for Liberty or any of the other workers there to seat him.

The moment he slid into the booth, Mara stiffened until she realized it was him sitting across from her. It was only then that she relaxed. Her mind was a million miles away.

"Luca? What are you doing here?" she gasped. Her hair was out of its usual bun. The long locks were curled perfectly at the ends. She had one side tucked behind her ear, and the other side hung loose concealing part of her face.

"I should ask you the same thing," he pressed, glancing around the bar at the men who were taking up most of the tables. "This isn't quite the place for a woman to be hanging out on her own."

"I disagree," she chuckled and jutted her chin out toward the main bar where several of the Shaw pride were taking up residence while their mates worked the night shift. "This place is crawling with panthers, and they wouldn't let anything happen to anyone. I trust them."

"I have to ask," he said, lowering his voice. "Are you one of them? And don't lie to me, Mara. I'm a shifter, and I have excellent senses. I know you are not human. That much is obvious."

"Not even close," she vowed, taking a sip of her beer. As her lips left the bottle, she gave him a soft smile. "I'm nothing like your kind."

"Are you going to tell me what you are?" he continued with the questions. He had to know. "Your scent…it's different than us."

Mara let out a long, boisterous laugh while she took another swing of her beer, "Luca, I'm sure my origins come from the fiery pits of hell."

"A demon?" he barked, going on the defense.

"Hold your anger, Luca," she said with a roll of her eyes. "I am not a demon, and I'm not here to cause problems. I want to live in peace."

"You still didn't answer my question," he reminded her. "What are you?"

"I know you've heard the old saying, 'A woman never tells her secrets', right?"

Luca nodded.

"Well, my secret is my own. I promise you that I'm not here to harm anyone or anything," she sighed. "I honestly like being alone." She was lying, and he knew it by the way her eyes cut away from him. Plus, the scent of it burned his nose.

"From the look on your face, I have to disagree," he pressed. She looked so sad…like she was choosing a life she didn't want to live.

"I just need you to trust me," she added. "I am weak, and I will always be like this unless I give into my supernatural behavior. I guarantee that will *never* happen in this town."

Mating Scent

"Why not?" Damn, he was so curious as to what she was, and she wasn't giving him anything he could go on.

"Because I like it here." She shrugged. "That's it. I'm not hiding from anyone, nor am I going to be hunted. Yes, there are people out there who want me to join them, but it's not a rule. No one *owns* me. I can do as I please. Can you just accept that and let me have my dinner in peace?"

Yeah, well, the more he scented her, the more his bear wanted to own her in every way. But his human side wasn't about to touch her to see if she was his mate. It was obvious she wanted to be left alone.

"I'm sorry for intruding, and since you want to be alone, I will take my leave," he said in defeat, but with an air of respect. "However, if you ever get into a situation, I want you to contact me." He had a pen in his back pocket and scribbled his phone number on an unused napkin, sliding it over. "Add me to your phone before the night is over."

"Thank you, Luca." She nodded and folded the napkin up before sliding it into the inside pocket of her jacket. "I'll keep that in mind."

"Have a good rest of your evening," he offered as he slid out of the booth. He never looked back, but he could feel her eyes on him as he walked away.

And that was the moment everything changed for him.

Luca wanted to know more, and his next stop was to see Gaia.

When he pulled up to her little house on the lake, she had already stepped out onto the porch. Even though he'd only known her for two years, she'd become a mother to him, just like she'd done with the Morgan brothers.

The closer he got to her doorstep, the sadder her face became. "Gaia?"

"Come inside, son," she sighed. Gaia was in her mid-forties…well, her human body was. He knew she was millions of years old, though. "Take a seat. I'll get you a beer. It appears you need one."

"Thank you," he replied as he moved over to her couch. Within a few seconds, she shoved an ice-cold bottle in his hand.

"Talk," she ordered.

"It's Mara," he began, taking a long pull off of the beer. "I saw her tonight at The Deuce, and my instincts went straight to her being alone. She told me she was fine, but her scent…it's been driving me crazy trying to figure out *what* she is, because she isn't a shifter or human. I came over here to see if you could tell me."

"Ah," she frowned, leaning back in her chair. "That isn't my story to tell."

"Is she dangerous? I need to know if she is going to come for my family," Luca asked, because he didn't want any more death to come to their doors. He'd been through enough, already.

"Son," Gaia said, placing her hand over his. She wasn't going to burn because she wasn't mated, and for some reason, with her being the mother of the earth, she could touch anyone she wanted without any repercussions. "I can't promise anything when it comes to Mara, but I can tell you that you should probably get

Mating Scent

to know her better. With time and trust, she will come out of her shell."

"She's my mate?" he gasped, realizing what Gaia was hinting at.

"Just get to know her, and please, go easy with her," Gaia urged. "She's going to need you, and you are going to need her."

"Now you are a psychic?" he laughed.

"I know things." Gaia tapped the side of her head like she had more sense than even the smartest humans on the planet.

"Then tell me," he urged, squeezing her hand. "I have to know everything about her."

"I can't betray anyone…not even for you, my dear Luca," she began, standing up to walk away. Luca was about to ask her what she was doing, but he knew it was probably for the best.

She tore off a sheet of paper from a tiny notepad and folded it in half. The look on her face said she didn't want to give it to him, but she held out her hand anyway. "Here's her address. Take it easy with her, and do not touch her without her consent."

Luca unfolded the paper and memorized the address, realizing Mara didn't live far from Gaia.

"I would never do that to a female," he growled. "Even though I was raised in that shithole by my uncle, I still kept my respect for women and our kind."

"I know you did, honey," she whispered, walking up to him to place her hand on his cheek. She closed her eyes, and Luca felt the warm winds she'd sent through his body, relaxing him. "Take care of that female…she's going to need you."

Mara was a few days out from her piddly blood bag of shifter blood, but she felt stronger already. It wasn't the strength she needed to be herself, because she hadn't drunk right from the source. A human usually held ten pints, and if she took five from a shifter, they could regenerate their blood in a matter of seconds after shifting.

Five pints would hold her over for a month…maybe six weeks.

She'd only had two. To a vampire, that was like eating half of an orange. It would give them enough to soothe the hunger for a little while, but it didn't quite give them all the vitamins and strength they needed to do anything else in their lives.

She tried to go to The Deuce the other night, looking for any shifters who might not have alphas or mates, but she left empty-handed.

Except for Luca O'Kelly.

He was a bear with no alpha, and he wasn't mated.

The perfect snack.

There was the scent he gave off whenever they were close. It was unique; forest, manliness, safety, and protection. It was a mating scent, but not strong enough to know for sure.

She let him leave her at the booth, and she finished her beer before going home. The next two days were hell. He didn't come in for meals at the diner, and she

Mating Scent

knew they were working hard in their fields, but another part of her was upset he didn't even stop by.

Mara shook her head to dislodge the thoughts. He wouldn't be willing to feed her anyway. That was just too much to ask of him. He was a worthy male; unlike the others she'd fed from over the last ten years. Those nasty bears liked her bite. They'd do anything for her like she was a damn siren or something.

And she hated it.

All she wanted was to find a mate, one that accepted her for who she was. If he gave her his vein, she wanted him to give it to help her live…not because of how good the male's release was while her teeth were buried in his neck.

After all of her travels, and after all of the locations she'd lived, she'd never found a willing bear to give her his blood without some type of repayment. They always wanted sex, but she just needed to feed.

It made her feel dirty and used.

She wanted a male who would offer himself to her without any questions or sexual favors in return. If she did find that type of mate, she was sure the sexual part would come into play while she fed, and that was okay with her…but *only* because of their connection and love.

She was a fucking vampire.

Could she ever find true love as a vampire? In her eyes, she was a joke created by the devil to disrupt the gods.

A freak of nature.

A demon from hell.

A vampire who craved the taste of the blood from a

shifter created by the gods.

It was time for her to accept her fate. Since her blood dealer was having a hard time finding and packaging shifter blood to ship to her, there would be some changes coming her way in the next week.

She would weaken and lose even more weight.

As it was, she was barely one hundred and twenty pounds. At her best, when she was able to feed off of the men who used her body, she weighed a good thirty pounds more.

She took a shower and spent the longest time looking at herself in the mirror. Her body was still shaped in a seductive way, but there were changes. Her ribs were exposed, and she hated that her stomach was concaved, making her bones more pronounced.

Her breasts weren't the same. Mara had to chuckle because she hated them being so big when she was at the height of great health. Smaller breasts fit her well. She laughed again until it died on her tongue when she got to her hips.

She took her finger and poked at her tiny legs and bony hips. There wasn't an ounce of fat on them, and she hated it. *Fuck*, she thought. Most women hated their bodies when they were beautiful and full. She was hating on her own for being skinny. She looked anorexic.

Her eyes were starting to show dark circles and her cheekbones were getting more and more pronounced. Thankfully, there was a lot of makeup out there that she could use to contour her face to make it look more natural.

Mating Scent

The only thing that would sell her out was if she scented shifter blood.

If she did, it could turn her eyes red and her fangs would grow in her mouth. At that point, her secret would be out there for the world to know if she couldn't fight off the frenzy of her nature when shifter blood was spilled.

And she couldn't have that.

Thankfully, she hadn't experienced it since moving to Olive Branch.

And she prayed to whatever gods were out there to thank them for helping her keep her cover.

She didn't want to trade shifter blood for sex ever again. If she were to have a perfect male to feed her, she would be stronger than any shifter out there. Her body would be full and her strength would be that of a thousand men.

To be honest, that knowledge scared the fuck out of her.

She never wanted to hurt anyone.

Not now…not ever.

Especially, not Luca O'Kelly.

Chapter 5

Luca was fed the fuck up.

It'd been almost six days since he'd laid eyes on Mara Wood.

Basically, a freaking week!

All of the seeds were planted, and although he was thinking about her, he had to help the females build their little garden just out the back door.

"I'm ready for three more bags of soil, Luca," Ada called out over her shoulder.

He chuckled to himself and walked toward the barn where Rex was repairing some equipment. Drake and Tessa were missing, and he didn't even want to ask where they were.

"Mate need more soil?" Rex asked.

"Three bags for now," Luca rolled his eyes. "The

elders are out there helping, too."

The elders, who were in their seventies, loved taking care of the gardens with the mates. Although Peggy and Alfred Martin and Martha and Doug Downs were in their early seventies, they worked hard and helped provide for the clan. They were loving friends to all of the clan, especially the female mates. They taught them valuable lessons about living off the land, and Anna Claire had held a special place in their hearts because of the hell she'd endured at the hands of her father.

When he dropped off the soil, everyone dug into them, splitting the bags to fill the raised bed for the new herb garden. The rest went into the main garden for tomatoes, okra, and other vegetables they ate on the regular.

Anna Claire was breathing heavier than the others when she picked up a bag, and Luca narrowed his eyes. It didn't take long for her scent to reach him, and he rushed over to grab the bag off her shoulder.

"You're with young?" His question was more like a statement, and she lowered her eyes.

"Gunnar knows, and I promised him I was fine. I'm also promising you that I am okay. Just because I'm with young doesn't mean I'm going to sit out this spring and not help. So, keep your manly opinions to yourself."

"Yes, Ma'am!" Luca's eyes widened and his hands went in the air. "Whatever you say, but I'm not getting blamed if you overdo it."

"I'm fine," she huffed. "If he says anything to you, I want to know. I'm not in any mood to deal with his overprotective bullshit."

"I'll grab one extra bag of soil for you," he said, using the excuse to get out of the area. Anna Claire was not in the mood today, and he didn't blame her. He may have only been at the Morgan clan for two years, but he knew how protective the brothers were of their mates.

By the time he reached the barn, Rex was moving a piece of equipment out and jumping into another one to do whatever maintenance was needed. Luca took that opportunity to grab what he needed and get the hell out of there. He didn't want to hear Rex ask about his mate, either. Sometimes, hearing their overbearing protective words made him roll his eyes. Then, they would preach to him about when he found his mate. They said he'd be the same way.

Once his job was done, Luca snuck off to his cabin. He had to look up information on the web about paranormal creatures who weren't bears or panther shifters, but he didn't find anything of use. Hell, after the last few years, knowing the Shaw pride, he'd learned a few things about the wolves, too. However, she didn't scent of a wolf.

But Mara was different than everyone else. There was no doubting it.

Whatever she was, he was going to make it his mission to figure her out.

After he did a quick drive-by to check the fields, Luca made his way over to the diner, hoping she was there, and sure enough, the beautiful female met him at the door. His mating scent amplified, and so did hers.

"Morning, Luca," she greeted. "Table or booth?"

"It's just me today," he replied. "Can I sit at the breakfast bar? It looks empty enough."

"Of course, you can," she replied with a smile. "Follow me."

Yeah, following her was a bad idea. Even as tiny as she was, her body had curves that made his mouth water for more than food. He imagined using his tongue to taste every inch of her body.

"I'll bring you some coffee while you look at the menu," she said, placing the plastic-coated menu in front of him.

He looked over the menu while she flitted around, refilling coffee for the humans in the diner. When she returned to take his order, his mouth opened, and what came out wasn't his order.

"Let me take you out to dinner tonight," he blurted, his eyes narrowing to focus on her expression. She wasn't shocked, nor was she appalled. That had to be a good sign, right?

"Oh, Luca," she finally said after a moment of hesitation. "I'm not the female for you."

"You're different, and I know you know what I am," he growled. "My beast and I can't stop thinking about you. I'm not asking you to mate me, or even touch me. I just want to get to know you better."

Mara hesitated for a moment with a carafe in hand. The coffee inside of it vibrated from her shaking hands.

"Luca, as much as I want to say yes, there is a part of me that wants to say no," she admitted, finally setting the pot of coffee back on the burner to keep it warm. "It's best you stay away from me."

Mating Scent

"Mara." Her name dropped from his lips like a prayer. "Please. Just give me one date…one night."

She gave him a sad look. "I'll be back."

As he sipped the hot liquid, Luca watched her from the corner of his eye. She was very careful around the humans, and none of them touched her. He was glad, because the longer he and his beast were around her, the more protective they were becoming. If a male had touched her, he was certain his bear would've responded negatively.

Mara disappeared for a moment to serve food to a table. When she finally returned, she didn't look happy.

"Okay, fine, but I'm warning you," she narrowed her eyes. "I'm not the woman you should be courting."

She used old terms, and sometimes her mannerisms were too well put together like she'd been through some type of finishing school. He wanted…no needed…to know more about her. The ache he felt when he scented her had started to infiltrate his dreams, too.

"I will pick you up at six tonight."

"Tonight?" she gasped. "Like, tonight, tonight?"

"Yes, my dear…tonight," he smirked. "And I'd like to order the breakfast special, but add some extra gravy to the biscuits, please."

"Do you want my address?" she asked.

"I already know where you live." He grinned and took a sip of his coffee, looking at her over the rim of the cup. He wouldn't tell her Gaia had given him the address to her tiny house. Yes, he'd driven by it several times over the last few days, noting how quiet and empty it appeared from the road. "Dress casual."

He'd shaken her up, and he wasn't stupid. He knew exactly what he was doing.

Mara entered her tiny home not far from the diner. She had less than three hours before Luca showed up for their date. She couldn't control the tremors in her hands as her nerves fired. She was going on a date with a bear…a shifter. As much as it was a bad idea, Mara wanted to do it even though she was scared out of her mind over being alone with Luca O'Kelly. A quick glance in the mirror proved she had a lot of preparing to do before he arrived.

Why was she rushing? She had enough time, because she wasn't going to go to the extreme to look good for the werebear. In her vampire mind, he was food…nothing else.

Right?

And that was bullshit. She actually liked him. He was a dominant male…an alpha you could say, and he was honest. But he was also an asshole and had become even more bitter and jaded since his brother had been killed two years prior. But there was something about him that she liked. Luca didn't speak much, but when he did, he spoke his mind. Just like when he asked her out on the date.

This was going to be different than anything she'd experienced since being turned, and she knew it. How different? Like totally different?

It was obvious he liked her, and she'd be lying if she

said she didn't notice how amazingly hot he was. Ugh. Dear gods! Long hair on a male was always her weakness, but that probably came from her nature to feed on shifters. All bears kept their hair long. She didn't know why, but who cared anyway, right?

Shaking herself, she had to remember to resist the urge to feed. He was in his mating season. She was probably just a test for him, because he was looking for a mate.

She didn't think she was mating material.

Realization struck her as she reached for the last pint of her delivery. If she was going to actually go out on a date with a werebear, she needed to be under control. She ripped the tip off the little tube on the blood bag and moaned as her fangs grew in her mouth. It took every ounce of strength she had to not sink them into the bag. She had to suck the blood out like she was using a straw, and a part of her hated it. Her nature craved the feel of her fangs as they broke into the skin right at the life vein she was designed to feed from since she'd been turned.

But, the truth…yeah, the truth struck her so hard, she slid down the wall, blood bag in hand, and gasped. "I can't date him. I'll want to feed on him."

And she hated herself for wanting to feed on anyone…let alone a bear who could kill her with one bite of his massive bear teeth to her neck. He could rip her dead heart from her body just as easily.

Tears formed in her eyes. She felt like a fraud; going on a date with a werebear who had no idea what she was…or what he could be for her repressed nature.

Mara clenched her jaw and brought the bag back to her lips. The monthly deliveries would have to do. She didn't want anyone to know what she was, and as far as Luca? She'd complete the date to satisfy his need to search for his mate, knowing she wasn't going to be the one for him.

By the time she'd pulled herself together, she stood in front of the mirror and tried to look past her bony shoulders that stuck out like a beacon from the soft red halter dress she'd chosen for the night. She reached over and fumbled through her closet, grabbing a light denim jacket, sliding her arms through the sleeves. Once it was in place, she was somewhat satisfied with the coverage.

With what was left of her super hearing, the sounds of truck tires pulling in next to her car gave her a burst of energy and renewed nervousness. He was there to pick her up.

Mara flipped off the light to her bathroom and made her way to the door the moment she heard two knocks. He was a large male, but his knock was soft, and hearing that calmed her slightly.

She held her shoulders high and took a calming breath before opening the door. He was dressed in a pair of jeans that fit his muscular legs like they were made for him, black combat-style boots, and a dark blue, long-sleeved dress shirt.

As her eyes traveled from his feet up his thighs to his massive chest and long hair, she heard a growl low in his throat. The moment she got to what should've been his brown eyes, Mara took a step back as his face

Mating Scent

bubbled and his eyes glowed a golden color. It was the color of his bear.

"Luca?" she asked in fear. A sneer pulled his upper lip high, exposing his canines. "What's wrong?"

He moved toward her, and she took another step back, fear racing up her spine. Did he know what she was? Was he there to kill her? Oh, gods, what had she agreed to? Who told him?

"Stop, Luca," she barked, holding up her hand, but he took another step toward her with flared nostrils. "Luca!"

"You reek of another bear," he snarled. One shake of his head, his hair fluttering around his tight jaws, and he was completely changed. His eyes were a full golden color, and his canines were thick…impressively thick.

"What are you talking about?" she gasped, placing her hand on her chest. She might've been a vampire, but she was a weak one…easily disposed of, and that fear had tears building in her eyes. She hated being weak for the very reason she couldn't protect herself.

"I can sense a male bear covering your scent," he replied, gravitating in her direction. By that time, she was being herded into a corner. Mara's vampire nature was attempting to take hold of her body, but she used what strength she had to keep from revealing her true self.

Deep breath.
Grit your teeth.
Don't show your true self.

All of those mantras ran through her mind. There were dangers around each corner, and unless the shifters accepted her for what she truly was after her change, then she could be in trouble. Mara worried that any shifter who didn't know about her existence would be a problem, and by problem, it meant they could kill you.

"I haven't been around another bear in the area for almost a week!" she defended. Mara could feel the anger coming off Luca's body. How many lies could she tell him without him scenting her deceit? Bears had better senses than any other shifter out there. Wolves were a close second. So were the cougars.

"No, it's been today," he pressed, backing her toward wall. His hand came up and slammed into the wall above her head. Mara's body bumped into the wall, and she cowered under his golden gaze. "Who is it? Who touched you?"

"Why do you care?" she retorted, pushing away from the wall to make him step back while trying to keep from flashing her fangs at him. He still didn't know what she was, and she wanted to keep it that way. A part of her mind wanted to just admit it, but she wasn't sure it would go over well. "I'm not yours to protect or control. What I do on my own time is none of your fucking business, Luca."

Grizzlies became overbearing and growly in their mating season. It was obvious Luca was feeling the mating season particularly hard this spring.

"Oh, I care, and so does my bear," he replied. His eyes were not anything close to human at that point. They glowed…like shining a light on a brick of pure gold. "I want to know who you've been around that is not part of my clan, and don't lie to me, because I can scent it a mile away."

Realization hit her as she glanced at the empty blood bag in the trashcan right behind him. It was the scent of the male who'd donated his blood for her. *Fuck!*

"It's not what you think," she began, her voice shaking. She was found out. There was a sense of urgency to run, but something heavier held her body in place.

"What do you mean?" he snarled. "My bear and I are getting agitated. You better start explaining."

Luca was ruled by his mating season, and his unique scent was filling the air around her. With his angry gaze pinning her where she stood, she was trapped, and instead of feeling cornered, his scent and dominance was almost comforting.

A relieved breath rushed out of her lungs. Mara was caught, and when she should've run, she just…couldn't. How was she going to tell him? How? The words wouldn't come from her lips, but something deep…very deep inside her mind told her to stay.

Stay for him…stay for the male…Luca.

Her…*mate*?

"I'm waiting, my sweet Mara," he hummed.

"I can't, Luca," she choked, feeling the truth sitting on the tip of her tongue, but the fear choked her. "I just *can't* tell you. You'll hate me."

That was the wrong thing to say, because his eyes widened and his head tilted back on his shoulders and he roared so loud that it shook the entire tiny house. The vibrations rattled her chest, and she was drawn to him…his roar…his scent.

"I could never hate you, Mara," he finally said after he'd taken three or four deep breaths to calm himself and his beast. "Tell me. I promise not to judge you. I swear it."

She couldn't bring the words to her lips. He would hate her. He might even try to kill her…

But there was something there…in his eyes.

"Mara, I know you are not entirely human," he admitted. "Whatever you are…it's okay."

No, no it wasn't. She didn't want to be discovered, and she told him as much. "Luca, as much as I want to tell you, I'm scared. I don't want anyone to know."

"Why?" he asked, his eyes darkening again. "Is someone looking for you? Who is it? I want to know because I will find them and kill them."

"No," she shook her head. "No, it's not like that. I'm different. I'm…I'm nothing like you…I wasn't made by the gods."

"What are you talking about?" He was getting more and more agitated by the second, and his scent was scrambling her mind. Gods, it was so strong. Strong like his physical appearance…muscular…manly…beastly.

"I'm a product of hell, Luca. I swear, I was created…well, turned, really. My kind are the ones who were created to piss off the gods. I…I…" *Fuck!* She mentioned that she was a turned beast. The words had slipped from her mouth. She was going to have to tell him, because Mara had a feeling he wouldn't leave until he knew the truth.

"Tell me, damn it!" Luca smacked the wall above her

Mating Scent

head after overpowering her with his size and backing her into the wall, again.

"I'm so sorry," she cried, covering her face. She had to tell him. "Luca, I'm a vampire, and I have to feed on shifters to live. I don't feed on your kind, though. I have a supplier who sends me small amounts of blood every month. I drank from a blood bag before you got here to give myself just enough strength to be able to handle our date. I didn't want to crave you, and I didn't want to even *think* about feeding off of you. The scent you caught when the door opened was the donor bear's blood."

"The what?" he asked, pushing away from the wall. Mara tried to hold her tears at his rejection, but she knew this would be the outcome. "You drank blood from another male of my species?"

"I'm sorry, Luca," she sniffled. "I know it's a shock, and I won't be mad if you leave. I just ask that you keep my secret. I want to live here and be a normal human…for once. If I keep suppressing my need to feed, I can be almost human again. Feeding off a shifter would make me too strong…stronger than even you."

"Mara," he breathed, moving back into her personal space after the shock of her admission sent him back a step. She didn't blame him for his reaction. "Look at me."

She couldn't bring herself to raise her chin, and she knew he wouldn't touch her to force it. But there was a need there. To look into his eyes…and she didn't know if it was her vampire senses or his scent that told her he would touch her regardless.

When she did, his face was framed by his hair,

hanging perfectly to show the sharpness of his jaw and highlight the golden color of his eyes. Luca's breaths were coming out harshly, but for some reason, it was comforting, yet scary…like a predator waiting for the chance to pounce.

"Explain your kind to me." It wasn't a question, and while he still hovered, she felt a connection to him, and her mouth opened. It didn't take long for her to spill everything about herself.

"Luca, please," she swallowed. "You have to listen to me. I am a vampire, but not like what you think or even know. As far as I know from the stories passed down over the last thousand years, hell made my kind to piss off the gods. However, I've only been this way for ten years. I don't know everything about what we are, but what I've learned is that I can feed on a willing shifter to survive. If I suppress my need, I grow weak. I lose weight, but I won't die. It will make me damn near human again, but I still crave blood. I've gotten really good about repressing my nature. The shipments I get from my source are scattered. Some months, I get enough bags to help me live without being too weak to get out of bed, but this month, I only had two bags arrive. I drank it tonight to give me enough strength to be able to dress up for this date and not have to use makeup to cover the dark circles around my eyes."

"I've never heard of a vampire that feeds off of shifters," he said, pushing away from the wall again. "I thought vampires were a myth."

"Weren't you a myth at one point?" she asked, taking a step away from the wall when he moved far

Mating Scent

enough to give her some breathing room.

Mara ignored his golden eyes and got some distance from him. She took a seat on her couch, running her hand through her long, dark hair. Her anxiety was at its highest since she'd fled her maker. Dropping her hand to her lap, she forced herself to stop the nervous tic she had for finger-combing her hair. Her paranoia and anxiety got the best of her, showing her tell-tale sign of weakness.

"I know this is a shock, and from what I understand, there are not a lot of us, because we usually stay hidden…or we find clans that accept us and keep us at their homes because we work for them in exchange for blood donations." She wasn't going to tell him about the ones who wanted sex in return for their vein yet.

Luca was agitated, and Mara could feel it like the heat from a raging fire. She had no idea that she could connect to a male like that. There was something brewing inside her vampire body she didn't understand, and she had a feeling it had something to do with the scent coming from his pores.

"How weak are you?" he grunted, looking her dead on in the eyes.

"I tell you I'm a vampire who could use you as a snack, and you're worried if I'm hungry?" she chuckled. What was he thinking? When she realized what he was asking, she immediately started shaking her head. "I will not feed on you. Not when you are in the height of mating season."

"Oh, my dear Mara," he huffed, narrowing his golden eyes. "Can you not scent me?"

"I have," she admitted, but she was too afraid to inhale in front of him. He was being dominant again, and as much as she liked to be on her own, she wanted more.

"Take a deep breath," he ordered. No, *demanded*.

Those golden eyes and his hardened face…it caused a stirring inside that created heat from her core all the way up her malnourished body. She closed her eyes and did as she was told.

His scent…the mating scent…was strong, overpowering, and sent wetness between her legs.

"It's your mating season," she swallowed. "Your scent is going to be stronger during the spring. I've lived with enough bears to know that is a normal part of your nature. It's spring, and you will be searching for a mate until the Summer Solstice."

"That's where you are wrong," he growled, closing the distance between them. He fell to his knees at her feet, and she immediately drew them up under her as she sat on the couch. "My mating scent only comes out when I'm around my mate, and from the scent now overpowering that male's blood, it tells me you are aroused by it. You can't lie to me, Mara Woods. I can taste it in the air."

"What?" It didn't take much for her to blush since she was depleted of blood, but what she'd drank earlier immediately rushed to her face.

"You're my mate."

"Me being your mate comes with issues, Luca," she sighed. "As a shifter-sucking vampire, I would have to feed on you to keep my strength. That's more than just

Mating Scent

a regular mating connection. Do you understand?"

"I don't understand everything," he admitted, and it made her cold, dead heart ache. "But, I'm willing to learn everything about your kind, if you teach me…tell me."

Luca's face finally returned to that of his human side, but his eyes still sparkled with golden specks in the dark brown. His beast was near, and she knew that. She'd been around enough grizzly shifters to sense and recognize their little hints as to when the bear was fighting with the human side.

"I can't be noticed here, Luca," she reminded him. "I want to live in peace. I don't want to have anyone who might be a hunter come for me."

"Vampire hunters?" he snarled, his eyes returning to the golden color that proved his nature. "There are humans who want you dead?"

"They are out there," she admitted with a nod.

"Where?" he asked. "Are there any in our area? I have to know so I can keep you safe."

"Not here," she promised with a raise of her hand. "After I killed the male who turned me, I fled, and I have been moving from place to place for the last few years. I finally found this town, and at first, I thought it was a normal, human town. I acquired a job with Gaia, and I began my new life. Then, the shifters started appearing for meals. I should've run, but I didn't. I love it here."

"You've been moving for years?" he asked with wide eyes. "You don't look more than twenty-three. How old are you?"

"Yeah," she sighed. "About that. I am immortal. This body hasn't aged since I was turned ten years ago."

"You don't age?" he pressed. She could see several questions spinning in his golden eyes.

"No."

Chapter 6

There was so much going on in Luca's mind at the moment, he couldn't process anything other than his bear had finally found its mate. Mara was his, and seeing the dark circles under her eyes and bones sticking from under her thin skin drove both of his sides insane.

"I want to touch you, but I can tell you are not even ready for that," he admitted. One thing he always promised himself was to be honest and never push his mate for a connection. It would always be up to her.

"I'm conflicted," she admitted, and he could scent her honesty in the air. There were no lies coming from her anymore. She was relaxing and telling him everything.

"I promised myself that I would never impulsively

touch my mate once my bear and I found her," he promised, holding up one hand as if it was a white flag. "Why don't we sit down again and talk this out?"

He pointed toward her couch. Gritting his teeth, he tried not to inhale her scent. It was driving his wild animal insane because she carried the stench of another male grizzly. He had to remind the beast she hadn't touched him.

Now, he had to understand her nature. She was a vampire. He'd heard whispers of them, but only of the ones who fed on humans, and as far as being a shifter, those vampires were not of his concern unless they started causing trouble for his clan.

But a vampire who only fed on shifter blood?

That could be bad.

"Tell me why you don't feed on shifters," he began once she found a comfortable place on the couch, tucking her legs under the beautiful, soft red dress she'd worn only for him and their date.

"Honestly?" she asked.

"Full honesty," he replied with a nod.

"Because…I don't want to be a sex object to a male who will give me his vein," she began, but stopped when his eyes glowed golden. "My whole life as a vampire has only been ten years. I found a few males who offered their vein while they used me for sex. As you know, for a male who is looking for a mate, the bite is addictive. But…I used them, and it made me feel wrong…dirty."

"Did they hurt you?" he snarled, moving closer. "If one of them touched you without your consent, I want their names! I will paint my face with their blood."

Mating Scent

"Luca, you have *got* to calm down," she urged. Her voice was a little harsh, but it worked to get his attention. He'd never seen Mara glare like that before, and he swore he saw a sprinkling of red in her blue eyes when she blurted her request.

"I don't want you to be alone here." Looking around her tiny home, he already saw several issues with her security. The back door was no thicker than cardboard and it wouldn't keep anyone out. There were no lights in the yard. She had no way of knowing if an enemy or a hunter was coming for her.

"I've been fine here for two years," she reminded him.

"Come home with me," he stated.

"What?" she scoffed, jumping to her feet. She folded her arms across her chest and leaned toward him. "No!"

"Until I know you are safe, *and fed*, I won't be able to stay away from you," he yelled, reaching for her as he bolted upright off the seat, but he dropped his hands to his sides. He wanted to touch her, tuck her away. She was so weak and fragile. "Mara, you are my mate and I can't protect you if you're not with me."

"But no one is coming for me!" she growled in return.

She stumbled back when her eyes filled with blood, taking over the sapphire blue he was growing to admire. Her hand reached for purchase, and he knew he was going to have to grab her if she didn't right herself.

"*Luca!*" she screamed as her hand slipped off the side of the end table.

With lightning-fast reflexes, his hand shot out and his fist bunched up in the front of her dress, pulling her upright without touching her skin.

She panted and looked down at his hand. Then, she glanced at the table. She would've cracked her skull if she'd hit it. "You saved me from hurting myself?"

"I did," he mumbled as he slowly opened his fist. His bear roared in his human mind for not touching her skin, but he'd refused to do that to a female who was destined to be his mate. "If you'd broken the skin, how bad would it have been?"

"I wouldn't have died," she cursed, turning away from him. Luca watched as she entered her little open kitchen and reached into the cabinet for a glass. She filled it with water and took a healthy sip. "Human food still gives me nourishment to make my organs function. Blood is what I need to be strong. If I'd spilled what little I have, I would've been too weak to get out of the bed until another shipment arrives next month."

"Do you make your own blood?" he asked.

"I don't know the science behind it, but from my understanding, yes…sort of," she shrugged, "The bear blood will mix with my own, giving me strength. I will then have regenerated my *own* blood."

"Genetically speaking, your blood changes depending on whom you feed from, correct?" he asked. What she was saying was so new to him, but he'd also secretly lived in a very remote Mississippi town for all of his life. The only thing from the big cities he ever saw were news reports of human bullshit that didn't involve him. However, he was a well-read male, and he'd read

Mating Scent

fictional stories of vampires in fantasy worlds. The authors liked to create their own worlds, but even as fiction, the mythology of a blood-sucking demon always had the same details…blood.

"Yes," she nodded.

"How weak are you now?" he asked, jutting his chin out toward her eyes. "Your eyes were red. Now, they're pink; slowly going back to that beautiful blue."

"You think my eyes are beautiful?" she asked. He couldn't tell if she was trying to blush or if it was her lack of blood.

"As a gemstone," he agreed with a nod, but his mind was churning. "Are you hungry?"

"That's a loaded question, Luca."

He didn't have to touch her to help her. She needed nourishment, and he was willing even if he didn't want to touch her. He jutted his chin out toward the end table where a glass sat. "Dump the water out of that glass and set it down on your kitchen table."

Luca didn't wait for her to ask him why, he just walked over to one of the chairs and pulled it out, taking a seat. Flicking the button at his wrist, he started rolling up his sleeve. He ignored her quick intake of air as she set the glass down.

"I can't ask that of you, Luca." She tried to wave her hands out in front of her to get his attention, but he brought his wrist to his mouth and used his growing canines to bite into his flesh.

"Sit down before you fall down, Mara," he said, using his foot to push out the chair across the table.

He turned his wrist over and let his blood drip into

the glass, scoring his vein again when his superhuman healing closed the wound. When he glanced at her, Mara had covered her mouth with her hands and her eyes were turning pink again. He didn't know how much he should give her…or even if he should be doing that, knowing they were mates.

The touch was one thing, but even shifters did a blood exchange during their mating rituals.

When his wrist healed on its own for the third time, Luca bit into it again until he had half a glass. She was still covering her mouth, and knowing she was hiding her fangs from him caused his own to thicken even more.

"Don't hide them from me," he ordered, pushing the glass toward the center of the table. "Now, drink this before it gets too cold."

Luca's heart crumbled when she snatched the glass and brought it to her mouth. He heard her fangs clink against the material as she gulped it down like she'd been living in a desert for the last ten years.

Remembering where she'd gotten the glass, he stood and found another one, identical to the one she was using. He bit into his wrist and started the procedure again. Once she set that one down, her nature forced her to reach for the refill.

"That's enough," she mumbled around the second glass when he began to bring his wrist to his lips for a third serving. "Too much won't be good. It'll change me. I can't do that."

"Change you?" he asked, his brows pinching forward.

Mating Scent

Gods, her hair was already so beautiful and styled with soft curls. Her face hadn't changed other than her eyes and fangs. What would change?

"It will make me gain weight," she panted as she finished the second glass. When he rolled his eyes, she cracked a smile, and his bear liked seeing its blood staining her fangs.

"All women say that," he chuckled. "You are as light as a feather, Mara."

"Yeah, but if I go into work tomorrow weighing twenty pounds heavier, people will start asking questions." Mara took the glasses to the sink and washed them out. "Drinking blood keeps me strong. Do you remember me telling you that?"

"Yes," he nodded, unsure of where she was going with her story.

"At my best, when I am able to drink enough blood to sustain what I am, I look like an athlete...like I keep my body toned for some type of competition. I'm *strong,* Luca. Dangerously strong."

"You need to be strong," he agreed. "You need to be able to protect yourself when I'm not around to protect you."

"I don't think you understand what I'm saying," she sighed, walking over to place her hands on the back of the chair. She took a deep breath and closed her eyes, but when they opened...Mara's blood-red eyes were devilish and her body swelled slightly. Nothing like what she had described, but he noticed how her shoulders grew in size. Her face filled out, removing the dark circles under her eyes he'd come to think were normal for her.

With one side of her lip lifted in a snarl, flashing a fang, Mara made fists with both of her hands and the wood on the back of the chair cracked and splintered into tiny pieces. When she opened her hands, she held them out for him to see. The wood inside her hands was pummeled into dust.

"When I am fed completely, I'm stronger than any shifter out there. I'm dangerous, Luca. You must understand that."

***

She didn't want to drink anymore of his blood, because it tasted like something she'd never experienced. The small amount he'd provided her gave her enough strength to demonstrate just what she was trying to explain to him.

"The town will talk if I bulk up too much overnight," she explained, feeling her arms already thickening in the denim jacket she wore over her dress to hide her boney shoulders. She slipped it off and folded it over her forearm. "This jacket was loose on me right before you got here."

The blood moving through her body felt good. It was warm, and she hadn't felt warmth like that in a very long time. The blood bags she got from her supplier were kept cold. She hated it. Cold blood was disgusting and turned her stomach. She knew it wasn't natural to drink it that way, anyway.

"You're still too thin," he grunted, moving closer. He

inhaled and smiled. "You finally smell like me."

"I'm assuming that's a good thing?" she teased, actually giggling for the first time in what felt like forever.

"Always a good thing," he hummed. There was a yearning in his golden eyes, and she felt the sexual heat coming from his body. It was odd having his blood in her body, but not touching him.

"Luca, we haven't touched," she reminded him, but it only made him pause for a half-step when he began to push his chair back from the table.

"I don't know what's happening to me," he choked, shaking his head just the slightest. His long, dark hair flowed as he made the move, and it sent his mating scent into the air thicker than it already was.

"Could it be your blood in me?" she wondered aloud. She'd been around bear clans, and she recognized the male who'd found their mate. Luca was her mate. It was obvious now. There was no question about that anymore after taking his blood, and even though they'd done it backward, in a sense, she knew he was feeling the mating pull.

"I don't know, but my bear is under my skin right now," he swallowed…hard. "I need to touch you, but I don't want to do it without your permission.

"That's very noble of you," she agreed. "However, I have been around bear clans for years, Luca. I understand exactly what you're feeling. I've seen it with other grizzly shifters."

"It's hard," he admitted, fisting at his side. "You know nothing about me. You don't know my demons or the things I have been through."

"I do know," she sniffled, remembering hearing Gaia talking with the Morgan brothers about Luca's brother's death two years ago. "I have super hearing, and I accidentally walked past Gaia's office when they were talking about your brother's death. I am so sorry. I couldn't even imagine the pain you felt."

"We were a pair…inseparable," he choked out. "I miss him like a part of me has died. That's why I can't touch you. I feel guilt like no other."

Mara hadn't heard him speak of his brother since he'd died, and the admission of his guilt touched her in ways she'd suppressed over the last ten years. Her family was gone. She had some cousins, aunts, and uncles still living, but she would never contact them, because if she did, she could possibly blow her cover. It wasn't worth that, and they hadn't been close to them anyway.

Luca needed his closure for Ransom's death. That had been done years ago for her with her own family.

"Wouldn't he want you to be happy?" she asked, hoping the question didn't come across as too personal.

"I'm sure he would." He cleared his throat and looked at the time. "We should head out and find you some human food."

She didn't object and redressed in her jacket. Picking up her house key, she gave him a smile, "I'm ready to go." There would be time for them to talk about their families later. Tonight was supposed to be for them.

Luca was quite the gentleman, and she appreciated his chivalry as he held open the truck door and then again at the steakhouse. As the waiter approached, she scented him and knew the male was one of the panther shifters in the area. He was younger, and not a Guardian like most of the ones who came to the diner.

"Luca," the waiter nodded slightly.

"Beau," her date responded. There was a little tension in the air, but not enough that she sensed any harm coming from the panther.

Beau's eyes landed on hers, and he inhaled just the tiniest bit. She knew the male was scenting Luca on her skin. He rambled off a congratulation and asked for their order. Once he walked away, she relaxed in her seat.

"He thinks we mated," she whispered, keeping her voice low so the humans around them didn't eavesdrop. "Your offering earlier covered my natural scent."

"That's a good thing," Luca admitted, looking around the room. "I don't want anyone to think otherwise."

Mara knew there was going to be a time when he finally touched her skin, and she would be linked to him through his nature. As odd as her entire existence sounded, being a mate to a shifter male was her species' goal in life. The rare occasion she'd met another vampire like her, he'd been mated to a panther, and he was very strong.

She could touch him that night, and she would do it without hesitation. However, Mara was unsure if Luca was in the right headspace to take on a mate. He was still mourning the death of his brother.

"What's on your mind?" Luca shook her from her thoughts, and she gave him a warm smile. She didn't want to lie to him, but it was better that way.

"I feel really good, and I have you to thank for that," she answered.

"We can discuss all of this later, but for now, I want you to eat," he ordered as the waiter arrived with their food.

She giggled when another helper arrived with his second steak for Luca. He gave her an audible huff and a grumpy look, "I eat a lot."

"I can see that." She blushed when his grumpy features turned to something a little naughtier.

For the first time, he broke a smile and his eyes scanned her body from her breasts to her eyes. "A lot."

"Let's eat," she reminded him and picked up her fork. "Your food is getting cold."

Chapter 7

It took every ounce of the patience he had to take her back to the small home she lived in and not tuck her away at his cabin. It wasn't safe, and he knew it. Knowing she was as supernatural as him and just as strong, Luca used that knowledge to walk her to the door after their meal. She would be okay alone, but he didn't like it.

"I can be here in twenty minutes if you need me," he proclaimed, holding open the screen door while she unlocked the deadbolt.

There was still a stench of the donated blood she had received, and it made his beast roar inside his head. As far as Luca was concerned, touching her or not, his future mate would never go without. If he had to score his wrist a million times to keep her fed, he would.

"Thank you for dinner, Luca." She turned once she crossed her threshold and faced him.

A voice inside his head sounded like his brother telling him to be happy for once and touch the female, but he wasn't going to do it that night. They both needed time, and they needed it for different reasons.

"Lock up," he pressed. "We can talk about this more tomorrow. I'm not working the fields with the Morgan brothers and can come over if you'd like."

"I'm off work tomorrow, too," she blushed. Her smile was void of her fangs, and his bear wasn't happy. The thought of her sinking her fangs into his neck to mark him as her mate made his cock harder.

"I'll be over by nine," he noted. "Wear something comfortable. I want you to meet my family and come to my cabin. You might as well pack a bag while you're at it."

"That's awfully forward of you, Luca O'Kelly," she chuckled. "What if I don't want to stay with you?" He knew she was teasing, but he wanted her to understand what was happening…or what was going to happen once he got her to his cabin.

"I know you are my mate, because my bear is on edge." He grinned and gave her a wink. "At some point, I am going to touch you, and once I do, you won't leave my bed until I am done mating you in all ways, Mara Wood."

What little blood she had in her body rushed to her face, and she closed her eyes for the smallest second.

"I feel it…in your blood," she agreed. "I knew this would happen one day. I would find my mate and live

Mating Scent

happily ever after."

"That's what I'm offering you," he reminded. "Mara, go to bed and call me in the morning. I'll be up by six."

He took a step back, placed his hand over his heart as a sign of respect, and turned for his truck. Every step away from her hurt, and so did every mile between her and his new home on the Morgan clan's land.

By the time he'd reached his cabin, Luca was a ball of nerves.

"I've found my mate, and she's a vampire," he whispered as he closed the door to the outside world, feeling his brother's presence all around him, but it was fading fast. There wasn't any more sorrow or pain in the cabin.

A heavy fog of mourning lifted from the air inside, and that was when he knew Ransom had probably passed through the veil. It was superstitious as hell, but Luca believed in it. His brother wouldn't have abandoned him unless he knew Luca was content.

"No matter what…I will always miss you, my brother," he said into the empty cabin.

The next morning came quickly. He'd actually slept through the night even knowing the beautiful female was home alone. Male grizzlies were very protective, and he would even say they were the most protective of the shifters.

However, he wanted to take it slow with her. He wanted to know more information about her kind and explain how a mating with a shifter worked.

Luca wasn't surprised by vampires. He'd heard there were a few covens in the US, but he only knew them to feed on humans. And shifters stayed away from them. This new revelation of a vampire who only survived on shifter blood worried him. How many of them were out there?

Mara demonstrated how strong she was with just a cup or two of his shifter blood. Were those vampires supposed to be tied in with clans or prides? Or packs for that matter? It angered him that he'd been so sheltered in his old clan. His uncle was a tyrant, and it infuriated him that he couldn't go back and kill the son of a bitch again.

He needed information, and since he wasn't required to be in the fields that day, he made a decision to get with Mara and find out more. He wanted to know every inch of her body and mind. The more he'd been around her, the more his bear wanted her in his den.

To calm his nerves, Luca showered and dressed in casual clothes. He wasn't wanting to do anything else except be with Mara on her day off. He was going to insist she come to his clan, but first, he needed to talk to the Morgan family.

His text was simple and to the point, telling the males he needed to have a talk with them. There was no reason to lie to them about Mara, because once she came around, they would either scent him on her…or scent her as being something they'd never met before. If the latter was the case, it could be deadly for his future mate.

Once he arrived at the main house where the Morgan brothers lived with their mates, Drake, the oldest, opened the door with furrowed brows.

Mating Scent

"You wanted to have a meeting with us?"

"Yes, it's important," Luca advised as he stepped inside the back door. Everyone was already gathered...even the mates.

The females held their cubs with care as they waited in the front living room, holding them tight to their chests. Luca knew his words would probably cause a panic, but he had to tell them.

"I believe I have found my mate." He paused to look everyone in the eyes. "She is not like us...nor is she human."

A round of curses lit the room, but he held up his hand to calm them. "She is no threat to us."

"Who is it?" Anna Claire asked, coming to her feet. Her mate, Gunner, moved to her side for protection. There was no threat coming to the Morgan clan, and he needed to have their understanding.

"Please, bear with me while I explain," he begged.

The males came to their mates' side, protecting them as they should. Luca knew his news wouldn't be met with congratulations, but they needed to know. The fact that Mara was so weak without real blood worried him. She was so tiny, but once she'd taken some of his blood, she'd gained maybe a few pounds of muscle.

"I've met a female," he said, pausing to take a deep breath. "You know her from Gaia's diner. It's Mara."

"We adore her," Tessa cheered. "Oh, this is wonderful, Luca!"

"I'm not done." He halted her with a raised hand. As much as the females were smiling, his next admission would probably tear them to pieces.

"I don't know if anyone has ever heard of a vampire race who feeds on shifters," he began, but stopped them when they all gasped and the males' eyes glowed golden from their beasts' pushing at their body to shift and protect.

"A what?" Rex bellowed.

"Just let me finish," Luca barked.

"I agree," Tessa announced. "Let him speak."

"There are vampires out there that survive on shifter blood. Mara is one of those. Fortunately, she isn't like that. She has suppressed her nature and doesn't feed on our kind. She is small for a reason, and without shifter blood, she is vulnerable to any attack if someone is coming for her. She can't protect herself, because that type of vampire will recess back into their human state if they don't feed."

A round of questions were tossed in the air. He answered what he knew and made notes on the ones he didn't understand. Mara would be open with him, and he would eventually bring her to the clan's land, but he had to make sure his shifter family understood she would never feed on them.

"I scored my wrist and gave her my blood," he admitted. "The small amount she had changed everything about her. She was stronger…happier. That cupful from my vein gave her enough strength to show me that if she is fed properly, Mara would be strong enough to protect us. I've never heard, or seen, anything like it before."

"Is she a threat to us?" Drake Morgan asked, holding his mate close.

Mating Scent

"No, that's the strange thing." He shook his head in disbelief. "Mara would be a warrior like the panthers have Guardians."

"She's that strong?" Anna Claire asked.

"Stronger than all of us combined, but she can only do that if she sustains herself on the blood of a shifter."

"Did you touch her?" Rex asked with a confused look on his face. "Do you know for certain she is your mate?"

"I haven't touched her, yet. She drank my blood, and I saw the immediate change in her body. My bear approved of what I was doing. I think he would've given her every last drop in my body if she needed it."

"I've never heard of this type of vampire," Rex admitted, pushing away from where he was leaning against the wall. "I know there are small covens around the world that feed on humans, though. None of those are even close to us."

"Why is she here?" Ada asked.

"She wanted a normal life," Luca said, remembering how she scented of another male's blood when he'd arrived at her tiny house. "If she doesn't feed, she weakens. For the last two years, she's had someone shipping her pints of blood to keep her energy up, but it wasn't enough."

"What are you going to do?" It was Tessa's turn to ask her own questions.

"I really don't know," he replied. As he wiped his hand down his face in frustration, he knew whatever was going on with them was going to have to be discussed more, and then he would touch her. There was no question about that. He and his bear knew she was the one. He just needed to figure out how to proceed.

Chapter 8

Mara sent Luca a message early the next morning when Gaia had called her in a rush. The part-time waitress who covered two morning shifts a week had quit suddenly, and her boss was stuck with only her and Mara to man the diner. Poor Gaia had no one but the bears. They were her family, and it made Mara sad that she was the only person her boss trusted to work for her.

Mara set breakfast plates in front of two men who had been talking about their fishing trip the next day. They were making plans on where they thought the fish would be biting while the older man held a printed version of a local lake.

It made her miss her family. She'd loved to fish with her grandfather in the summers when she was out of school. He had a cabin on one of the lakes in her old hometown of Dallas, Texas. She sighed and went back to grab the coffee carafe for their refills, and a little pain crossed her heart at the memories of another life she once had before she'd been turned and forced to move to northern New York State.

There was no need to dwell on it, because there was nothing she could do about her situation. As she smiled at the two men, a new thought crossed her mind, and she wondered if Luca liked to fish when he wasn't working in the fields with the Morgan brothers.

She loved the outdoors, but since moving to town, she had only visited the walking trails at the local park when the walls of her tiny home were closing in on her. It was the beginning of spring and each day came with slightly warmer weather, and she wanted to get out and away from the monotonous life she'd created for herself.

"Mara," Gaia called out. "Would you unlock the back door for the delivery driver?"

"Yes, ma'am," she replied and hurried toward the kitchen. When she pushed open the door, a new driver was standing there with a piece of paper in his hand showing the inventory he was to drop off. It wasn't their usual guy.

A chill rolled up her spine, and her body went on alert. So much so that it shocked her. Her instincts hadn't been active in a long time. There was something about the human male that she didn't trust. He wreaked of deceit.

"If you'll sign this, I'll bring everything inside."

He appeared harmless, and he didn't act like he

was going to snatch her or anything. In fact, he looked like a dad; clean-cut, mid-forties with a touch of grey to his dark hair. Whatever it was she felt had to be off.

"Gaia will be right here to sign off on the delivery," Mara hedged, looking for an excuse to get her boss to the door. "She likes to double-check the inventory herself. Let me get her."

"No problem, Mara," the male said. She was about to ask him how he knew her name, but she remembered her name badge on her apron. Damn, she was jumpy today.

It could've been the boost of energy she had gotten from Luca's blood.

She excused herself and found Gaia ringing up a customer. "Could you sign for the delivery? It's a new guy, and…"

Her voice trailed off when she realized she was about to spill one of her secrets about what she was. She didn't want her boss to know she could sense things.

"I need to count it anyway." Gaia patted her shoulder and handed her the receipt and change for the man sitting at the bar. "Just give this gentleman his change and check on my tables for me."

Mara walked past the two locals who took up spots at the diner bar and when she reached the end, she had that feeling again. Something was wrong, and when she set the receipt and money on the counter, sliding it over to the customer, she realized he was giving off the same sense of doom she'd felt with the delivery driver.

"Thanks, ma'am," he said with a cheerful smile. At

that point, she knew she was losing it, because the human male gathered his things and walked out the door, jumping into a new blue SUV, and drove out of the lot at the same time she heard Gaia close and lock the back door.

And just as quickly as her senses had sparked with danger, it was gone.

"Everything okay?" Gaia asked when she returned to the counter.

"Yeah, yeah," Mara lied, shaking herself. "Just daydreaming."

Mara excused herself to make her rounds, collecting dirty dishes and cups from the people who'd finished their meals. The diner was thriving, but Mara couldn't shake the feeling she had about the delivery driver and the male at the counter.

Her world had been turned upside down when she agreed to a date with the male grizzly, Luca. She'd be lying if she said he wasn't the sexiest male she'd ever met. And while she was on the subject, she'd notice his scent amplified when he'd been draining his vein into a glass for her nourishment.

Mara had been around enough male grizzlies to know what that meant. It wasn't a secret that she was going to be Luca's mate, but she had a feeling he was trying to accept the fact she would need to feed from his vein to stay strong.

It was all fucked up, and she had questioned many times since being turned as to *why* the devil or gods made the vampires the way they were. What was so special about drinking blood? Who was responsible for

Mating Scent

her future as a blood-sucking demon?

She knew some things about her fate, but not everything. When she'd been with the other grizzly clan, she was there for protection, and since she'd been stronger than any of them with the amount of blood they'd donated, she had a feeling she was viewed as superior to them. They would do anything to have her at their side to protect them.

However, when news broke that shifters were no longer a myth and a real part of the world, they had wanted to keep her closer, and they became her jailer. She didn't want that. Free will was something she'd strived for, and her mother had burned it into her brain that she didn't need a man to validate who she was. She'd been raised to believe she could conquer anything, but since being turned, she felt like she was being used by the clans she'd found. They wanted her body, too.

That feeling wasn't there when she was with Luca. He wanted her for who she was…despite her need to drink his blood…or any shifter's blood, for that matter.

Mara wasn't unknowledgeable about their ways of mating. Skin-to-skin touch was the one thing that connected mates. The sex and biting were what solidified their connection.

Luca was her mate, and she'd tried to suppress her mating scent, but she couldn't stop her own sweet smell around him. After he gave her his blood, she knew he was her mate, and that scared the fuck out of her. Not many shifters knew of their kind, and the ones who did weren't like Luca.

She knew once they touched each other, she wouldn't be able to feed off any other shifter unless it was a female, and because of her beliefs, she wouldn't *ever* take the blood of a female shifter. They needed their strength to keep themselves safe since it was rumored they were the weaker sex. However, she'd known a lot of female grizzly shifters in the last ten years, and they were just as vicious as the males when it came to protecting their clan and cubs.

"My life is so complicated," she murmured to herself as she cleared a table.

As the day wore on, she was a little disappointed Luca hadn't come into the diner. By the time she was home, she'd convinced herself that the male wasn't going to show up that day. Why would he, anyway? She'd admitted as to what she was, and it wasn't the easiest news to process. If she was a shifter, and she'd been told of a shifter blood-sucking abomination, she'd have run, too.

To her surprise, he was sitting in his truck when she pulled into her driveway. The male was out of his vehicle, opening her door before she had a chance to do it herself.

"Welcome home," he grinned. "How was work?"

What was left of her dead heart pumped wildly at seeing the male standing there. She was stunned silent for a moment, and as those moments went on, his eyes narrowed.

"Talk to me, little vamp," he smirked. "Did you think I wouldn't come back?"

Could he read minds?

Mating Scent

"Little vamp?" she giggled, knowing she should've been offended, but coming from Luca, she thought it was…cute?

"Sorry," he shrugged, giving her another wicked grin.

There was something about knowing the male was destined to be her mate that didn't bother her for the endearment. Luca was caring and understanding.

"I'm sorry I had to bail on our day to go into work. I wasn't expecting you to come back," she admitted, sliding out of her car. He moved back two steps so they didn't make skin-to-skin contact.

"I will always be here," he admitted. "You are my mate."

"So your grizzly says," she teased. "What about you? The human you?"

"This conversation shouldn't be had in your driveway," he advised, casting a glance over his shoulder. "Mind if we go inside for this?"

Mara knew he was right and gave him a nod, grabbing her bag out of her car. Once she slung it over her shoulder, she took the lead to her front door where she used the key to unlock the door.

Only to be rushed by Luca, grabbing her by the hood on her light jacket. She was twisted and turned to place her body behind him.

"Get in your car!" he barked.

"Luca? What's going on?"

"Hunters? Humans…" he growled, slightly shifting his features to that of his beast. "They've been in your house. I can scent the gunpowder."

"What?" she gasped, placing her hand on her chest. Vampire hunters were not common, and they resided nowhere near Olive Branch. That was why she had chosen that tiny community to live in as a human. No one knew about her…or so she thought.

"Car! Now!" he barked one last time before rushing into her home to search for the people who'd been there while she was away.

With the energy she had left from the blood he'd given her, Mara used her supernatural speed to get back to her car and lock herself inside. She cranked the engine and waited. She hadn't been that scared in a long time.

Within seconds, he was leaving the house with glowing golden eyes. As he approached the car, his anger was felt through the glass of her window. It took her a few seconds to get the nerve to roll it down.

"Follow me," he snarled. "You're going home with me."

"Why?" she asked.

"There were humans in your home today, and I have a feeling they are looking for you. I'm assuming they were here to kill you."

She sputtered, but no words came from her mouth.

"Okay…okay," she replied. "How do I get to your house?"

"You stay on my ass and run any red lights that might stop you," he ordered. "I know the sheriff and he will understand if we get pulled over."

On her nod, he jumped in his truck and backed out of her driveway. She followed him as told, and it took

Mating Scent

almost twenty minutes before they turned into a nondescript gravel drive south of town. When the main house came into view, there was a log cabin that was probably occupied by his clan members…the Morgan Clan.

To the left of their main driveway, another gravel road led to a few cabins closer to the wooded area in the back. Two barns sat to the left of the road. She followed Luca to the first cabin just past a huge barn and several pieces of farm equipment she couldn't even name.

He pulled up to a small, white cabin on the left and killed the engine. Mara leaned toward the windshield and took in the area. There were trees behind his home, but the front was void of any landscaping. Simple. Bare.

When he opened her car door, she immediately stepped out, feeling like the weight of the last hour was lifted from her shoulders.

"Luca, I don't understand what happened at my house," she admitted.

"Come inside," he ordered, pointing to his cabin. "I'll explain everything, Mara."

What could he know that she didn't? He was new to her kind…new to the knowledge of a shifter bloodsucker.

Luca took a deep breath, finally releasing the stench that was human, gunpowder, and the bad intentions he'd scented in Mara's home. Someone had been there while she was at work, and his beast was livid. What would've happened if she'd been there when they broke in?

The thought of her being harmed sent him into a feral frenzy, but he suppressed his beast once he made sure the home was clear. The scent they'd left behind was too strong, and he knew it'd been only an hour or two since they'd been there.

Hunters. Human ones at that.

Humans won't take another person from me.

He'd know that scent anywhere. It wasn't the first time he'd come across hunters of his kind, and the ones inside her home had shared the same aroma as the ones who'd hunted his brother two years prior. There was a vinegary scent to humans when they were evil, and it burnt his nose whenever he scented it.

"Get inside," he barked, knowing he sounded harsh, but Mara's safety was at the top of his list. He wasn't playing around and knowing someone was after her just made his beast even angrier. He didn't need to be ruled by his animal at the moment, because she wasn't like him. Shifting into a grizzly wouldn't do him any good. He had to stay human and use his animal's strength to protect her.

Once the door was closed, he reached over and locked the deadbolt. That wasn't something he did very often since he could hear anyone coming to visit. The visitors he expected to come for her were not welcome, and he had to talk to the clan to make sure they were on alert, too.

Mara stood in the living area of his and his late brother's home. He noticed she was shivering, and it

Mating Scent

took everything he had to not bring her into his arms. They hadn't touched yet, and he hoped to do that soon. But with the presence of danger, he wasn't sure it was the right time.

"Let me get you a blanket," he mumbled, turning for Ransom's old room. It still scented of his brother even after two years. He yanked the comforter off the bed and brought it back down the hallway, handing it over to his future mate…a vampire.

"Thank you," she whispered and pulled it over her shoulders.

She looked paler than usual, and he wasn't sure if it was from fright or the lack of blood to keep her strong.

"Sit on the couch." He pointed toward the spot and turned for the kitchen. "I'll make you some hot tea." It might've been early spring, but the night temperatures were still chilly in the area.

When he returned, she reached for the cup, but he furrowed his brow and set it on the coffee table. "I'm sorry. I don't want to accidentally touch you."

"Why?" she asked with her head cocked to the side.

"Because if I touch you, we will mate as my kind does, and I don't think either of us are ready for that," he admitted, taking a seat in a recliner a few feet away from her.

"With the hunters in the area, wouldn't it be better if we did go ahead with the mating? I would be strong enough to protect you and your clan." Her shrug wasn't dismissive. It was more of a revelation of sorts.

It was true. She would be stronger than any shifter if she did feed from his vein. Just from her drinking a small amount of his blood, he knew it, and he accepted it. She was a superior race, and it showed. Vampires were stronger than anything the gods or devil ever made.

It was close to sundown once she finally relaxed. He pushed a remote across the table. "I have plenty of channels for you to find something to watch. I need to talk to my clan."

"Are they going to reject me?" she panicked.

"No," he promised, waving his hand in front of her. "They know about you already. I've spoken to them, and I know most of them already know you from the diner. I need to let them know what I scented at your home. We *will* protect you here."

"I don't need protection," she reminded him, but her shoulders dropped. "If I had enough blood, I could protect all of you."

"I won't let anyone on this land who would bring you harm. I may not be a Morgan, but this is my clan. We work together to make our lives here safe. You are a part of it now."

"If you say so," she sighed. "I'm exhausted, Luca." He knew her words were true when her eyes fluttered.

"Lay down and I will be back soon. Sleep, my little vamp." He smirked at the nickname he'd given her. "I'll be back as soon as I can. If you want to sleep in the bed, there is one right down the hall. It belonged to my brother."

The thought of putting his fated mate in his brother's bed should've upset him, but it didn't. There was still a part of Ransom that lived inside Luca. If his brother had been alive, he would've offered the same.

"I think I will retire to bed," she said, covering a yawn. "Today has been a long day."

"You get some sleep." He looked at his watch and realized it was close to eight at night. The day had gotten away from him already. "I'll be back shortly."

She took the comforter and padded down the hallway. He picked up his phone and sent a text to the Morgan brothers. Thankfully, they were still awake and in the kitchen at the main house.

On instinct, he tested the scents in the air when he left his cabin, and he found nothing out of the ordinary. Only the smell of dirt on the plows and fertilizer stored in the barn reached his nose. There were no humans in the area, and he would've known. After Ransom was killed, he always scented the air whenever he left his cabin or arrived from being away from the clan. The human's natural scent was etched into his brain, and he would kill any of them that might cross their land.

The light on the back porch was on, and he didn't even knock when he pushed the door open. He might've only been a member of the clan for a couple of years, but he knew those brothers were always available when times were hard. They would help him protect Mara.

"What's going on?" Drake, the oldest brother, asked.

"A lot," Luca sighed, pulling a chair out from their large dining table. "Sit. I need to tell you everything that happened tonight with Mara."

"Is she hurt?" Gunnar asked. His eyes glowed golden, but recessed back to their usual brown when

Luca held up his hand to stall his friend's anger.

"She is safe…at my cabin," he advised. None of the males made any move to act as if they were angered there was a vampire in his home, and it helped Luca relax a little more. He knew the importance of having a fated mate no matter their species. Tessa had been human when Drake had touched her, turning her at a later time. Love didn't always come from your own species.

"Good," Rex grunted. "She is to be your mate and should be in your care."

"I agree with you, and what I have to tell you will just solidify your comment." He paused to run his fingers through his hair. "I waited for Mara at her house so I could see her after her shift at the diner. When she arrived, I started to walk up to her door, but a human scent burned my nose. There was a distinct scent of gunpowder along with it. I sent her to the car and checked her home, but there was no one there. Nothing had been disturbed, but somehow, they had gotten inside. I brought her here for protection, and I wanted to let you know that she will be staying here until we find out who is hunting her."

Feminine gasps came from behind him, and when he turned around, Tessa, Ada, and Anna Claire were standing there with wide eyes and in different stages of shock and anger. Drake started to stand, but a hard glare from his mate put him right back in his seat at the head of the table.

"Where is she now?" Tessa demanded.

"At my cabin, sleeping," he replied.

Mating Scent

"Who would want to hurt her?" Ada asked, wiping a tear from her face. "She is the sweetest little thing."

When his gaze returned to the males, he saw they were more concerned about their mates and the possibility of Mara's problems coming to their lands.

"Might as well tell you everything I know about her and what might be going on," he said, standing from his seat and waving the females over to the table to sit down in the extra chairs.

Luca gave them every up-to-date detail he had on Mara, but he didn't know everything. He advised them about the shifter blood and the outcome of her drinking his blood once they were mates.

"So, she'd be stronger than any of us?" Gunnar asked with a respectful nod. "That could be of use to us."

"I'm not *using* Mara for anything," he growled, taking the male's statement as if he wanted to use Mara as a weapon.

"That's not what I'm saying," the youngest Morgan brother promised. "I'm saying that strength in numbers is always better. We've seen what happens when humans want us dead. If Mara can stand beside us in the event we have another attack, it would help us keep the clan protected. We have elders who are not as strong as they once were."

Gunnar was right. The elders were aging, and they didn't know how much time they had left with them. As it was, they were already in their seventies, and each year made them frailer like elderly humans. It was no secret that shifters lost most of their strength the older they became. They weren't immune to old age or the disease that affected their kind. Their healing process slowed down and eventually, they would succumb to the years they were on this earth.

"So, you haven't touched her, but you gave her some of your blood?" Anna Claire asked. She looked confused, and Luca wanted to be honest with them if Mara was going to stay at his cabin until he was sure there was no threat to her.

"I scored my wrist and put it in a cup for her," he noted.

"You need to mate her, Luca," Anna Claire scolded. "She can't live off of your blood like that. It's not natural for them."

"How do you know that?" Gunnar asked his mate with narrowed eyes.

"Ah, well." She blushed when everyone turned in her direction.

"Anna Claire?" Gunnar growled.

"Well, I might have seen something on the dark web when we were looking up information on the humans who'd used that chat room to communicate before attacking us two years ago. I didn't think anything of it, but there is a whole other chat room on there for people who hunt vampires."

"Show me," Luca ordered, coming to his cousin's side. "I need to see this."

"No!" Drake barked and pushed his chair back. "We will not access the dark web from my home again. Once was enough."

"What about the sheriff?" Tessa blurted. "He's helped us before, and he must already know about

Mating Scent

Mara. He's a freaking angel."

"I think we need to let Mara in on this discussion," Ada interrupted. "It's her who these people want. I know I would want to be privy to anything regarding my safety."

Drake grumbled under his breath, but Tessa shot him a glare. Everyone knew the oldest Morgan brother didn't care much for the lawman. Hell, Drake didn't care much for anyone outside of the clan.

"I agree with you, Ada," Luca said. "Let's gather in the morning, and I will call the sheriff myself. I also agree with Drake on that, because we don't want the feds coming our way for using the dark web. No one knows what might happen if there is too much activity around the land, and we already know most people outside our circle don't always have an understanding of us."

The clan was quiet for several moments before Drake decided to end the meeting with that information and told his mate to head to their quarters. Luca shook all of the males' hands as they passed him, but he stopped when Anna Claire came to his side.

"Did you at least pack her a bag of clothes before you brought her here?"

"We had to get out of there fast," he advised, kicking himself for not thinking of that. He should've given her a chance to gather things from her house, but at the time, scenting danger, he didn't want her anywhere near it.

"I bet we wear the same size. Let me gather a few things for her," Anna Claire offered. "Once we talk to the sheriff, maybe he can take her home to pack a more sustainable bag."

"Thank you," Luca said, relaxing just a bit. "I'll escort her wherever she needs to go."

He wasn't going to be able to sleep until they got to the bottom of who had been in her house. The more time he spent around her, the more protective he became. He'd seen it with the other males in the clan when they'd been concerned about their mates.

He couldn't shake the feeling that something was coming for her, and he wished he'd had his brother with him to help protect Mara. Together, they were a team, but now, Ransom was gone and Luca was left to do it on his own.

"Hey," Anna Claire whispered as she came to his side. She was a blood relative, and they could touch without causing her any pain. "Everything is going to be okay. We are here for you."

"I know you are," he replied when she ran her hand over his arm. "I love you, cousin."

"We all love you, Luca." She saddened, lowering her voice. "He would want you to be happy."

"I know," he sighed. "I know."

Chapter 9

The sheriff pulled into the gravel drive of the Morgan clan's home, seeing the males standing on their large porch as he approached the house. He had no idea why he'd been requested, but he knew it was important to them. They wouldn't call him unless it was.

He exited his patrol car and left his hands out where they could see them. He left his service weapon in his car. The grizzlies were volatile, and they would turn on you in a second. So, he kept his hands out of his pockets and stopped once he reached the first porch step.

"You wanted to see me?" he asked, trying to judge their expressions, but he couldn't. They were all stoic. Even Luca O'Kelly. He was the newest to join the clan, staying after his brother had been killed by human hunters two years ago almost to the day.

"Come inside," Drake grumbled. "What we need to ask of you is not meant for porch talk."

Garrett waited for the males to enter, and when they sat at their large kitchen table, their mates were already there. He was surprised to see Mara Wood in her own seat. How did the vampire girl get in with the bears?

"Mara?" he asked without thinking twice about uttering her name.

"Sheriff," she replied with a nod. Her face held too much fear, and her eyes looked like she hadn't slept much the night before.

"What's going on?" he blurted, refusing a chair offered to him. "I'd rather stand for this conversation."

His eyes fell on every one of the Morgan clan members. The elders were seated on the backside of the table closest to the back door.

"We have a problem, and we need your help," Luca stated, taking over the meeting. Garrett found that odd since Drake was usually the head of anything relating to the clan even if they didn't need an alpha to live like other shifters. There was a hierarchy in the family, and Drake was the oldest of the original owners of the clan.

"I'm assuming this has to do with Mara," the sheriff noted, getting down to the business at hand.

"Yes," she said, clearing her throat. "Last night, when I arrived home from work, Luca met me there, but he scented what we believe to be hunters."

Garrett held his composure. He thought only Gaia and he knew exactly what Mara was, but he had guessed that wrong. If they were going to be asking him for help, he needed to be open with them or they wouldn't trust him.

"So, they know what you are?" he asked, holding up his hand when everyone in the room growled deathly low in their throats. "I knew what you were the moment I saw you at the diner for the first time, and since there have been no deaths by vampires in my town, I never confronted you."

"I guess I should say thank you for that." She relaxed. "I didn't come here to hurt anyone. I just wanted to live a normal life."

"Tell me about these hunters you scented?" Garrett asked.

Luca went into the short story of what he'd scented at Mara's house. Garrett didn't show any emotions when he realized that was just a quarter-mile from Gaia's home.

"We want access to the dark web," Tessa suggested. "There is some information on vampires in there that Anna Claire noticed a couple of years ago when we secretly looked for information on the human males who were plotting to kill us."

"The dark web is something you do not want to access," he reminded them.

"You have the right as a lawman to get on and look for the information we need," Mara stated. "I know there are hunters out there who come for vampires like me who feed on shifter blood and the ones who are draining humans in other parts of the world. I really need to know if someone has come to Olive Branch because they were tipped off about me."

"Who would tip them off?" Garrett asked, keeping the information he was getting in his mind and not on a notepad. Shifter business was to be kept secret for their safety, and that extended to other paranormal species.

"I don't know," she cursed. "I killed my maker and fled. I covered my tracks and haven't had any problems since I got here two years ago."

"I will access it, but I need Anna Claire to explain more about where she saw the information. Would you be willing to come to the department, after hours, of course?"

Anna Claire glanced at Gunnar, her mate, and ignored his harsh features. None of those bears would want to be seen anywhere near the sheriff's office. "What time?"

"No, absolutely not," Gunnar broke his silence, slashing his hand through the air. "It's too dangerous."

"I assure you, she will be protected, and I would expect you to escort her there," Garrett stated. "The town square closes its shops by eight. I can meet you at the side of the building at ten. I'll make sure the cameras and any officers mingling around do not see you."

"I want to help. It's the least I can do, Gunnar," she pleaded. "If something isn't right, we can drive off."

"No one sees us," Gunnar ordered, pointing at him. "And Luca has to come with us, too. If something happens to my mate, he is blood-related. If she needs to be touched, he can get her out of there should I have to defend us."

"Done," Garrett agreed to his terms. "Tonight, ten on

Mating Scent

the dot."

"We will be there," Gunnar confirmed.

"I should go with you," Mara begged Luca.

"It's too dangerous, and you are not strong enough yet," he reminded her. The blood he'd shared with her was quickly fading, and Luca knew her strength was waning by how much weight she'd lost overnight.

Luca prepared for the visit to the sheriff's office by pulling his long hair up with a tie, covering his head with a baseball cap. They were taking all precautions to not be seen by anyone who might recognize them.

"I'm going to get more blood shipped to me," she advised, but her breath held when he felt his eyes immediately turn golden. "I need to feed soon, or I won't be able to hold a tray of food. I'll be weak."

"You will drink from me when I mate you," he growled. "I'd touch your skin right this second if I could, but we wouldn't be leaving this cabin for three days while I made love to you as my mate. We will get the information on whoever it was that came to your house, and I will find them and lay their bodies at your feet."

Luca wasn't lying. He would do exactly what he said he'd do once he found the hunters. He scooped up a lightweight jacket off the hook behind his front door and tried not to notice Ransom's winter coat that he'd never removed after his brother's death.

"That's very protective of you, but I need all of the information, as well," she reminded him. "It is my life they're after." Mara was right, but he had to keep the people to a minimum going into the sheriff's office building. Drake and Rex were staying on the property to make rounds while the others were gone.

"While I'm gone, I'm going to take you up to the main house so you can sit with Tessa and Ada. Their mates will protect you until I can return," he advised, reaching for the door handle. When he looked over his shoulder, he saw the dark circles under her eyes, and he felt a pain in his chest that she was suffering without blood.

"Wait, before we go," he began. "Come to the kitchen."

"Luca, you don't have to do that now." She winced when he reached for a glass.

He bit into his wrist and held it out over the glass, cursing when his healing abilities closed the wound. Mara tried to stop him, but her eyes were changing to a faint pink color at the scent of his blood. He repeated the bite two more times before he handed over the glass. "Drink."

The appeal of his offering was too much for her to resist, and even though recently learning of her kind should've worried him, he wasn't the least bit put off by her need for blood. In fact, it aroused him, knowing she was consuming a part of him to keep her fed and strong.

"Thank you," she breathed after setting the glass down on the counter before he scooped it up and took it to the kitchen sink. He rinsed the glass off and stuck it on the top rack of his dishwasher.

"Feel better?" he asked, seeing the pink in her eyes

had already changed to red. "How long do your eyes stay red like that?"

"I do. Thank you. The red will stay a little while after I've fed. Maybe, a few minutes if I don't force them to change," she admitted, blinking a few times, and the next time she opened them, they were back to her regular color. Her fangs were recessed, too. To anyone else, she looked like a normal twenty-three-year-old female. She might've passed for a college student with her long brown hair that she kept slightly curled on the ends when she wasn't at work where Gaia required her to pin it up.

"Are you ready to go?" he asked, making sure she didn't need anything else.

"I need some clothes from my house." She frowned, looking down at the work shirt she still wore when she'd arrived home from work.

"Anna Claire is your size, and she has laid out a few things for you to use," he admitted. "As soon as I know your home is safe, I will take you over there to pack a more substantial suitcase."

She stared at him for a few seconds as if she was weighing her words. If it wasn't getting so late, Luca would ask her what she was thinking. "We can talk more tomorrow."

"I have to work tomorrow," she said once they left the cabin. The walk to the Morgan brother's home didn't take long.

"Gaia gave you the day off. I called her personally."

She stopped in her tracks, and he almost ran into her.

"You didn't tell her what I was or what's going on, did you?" Mara's eyes were as wide as saucers, and Luca had to remember that Mara didn't even know who her boss truly was.

"Again, tomorrow we will talk," he repeated. Waving his hand out in front of him to get her going again, he took a deep breath. "There's a lot you may not know about this place and the people who reside here."

"Let me guess," she huffed. "Answers are for tomorrow."

He gave her one nod and walked ahead to get the door, knowing tomorrow was going to be full of information for her. It was also time for Gaia to come clean about her true identity.

The females rushed over to offer her hugs and spoke to her in hushed tones, reassuring her everything was going to be okay. Tessa promised she was safe there, and offered to make her some human food.

"That would be great, thank you," Mara replied as Gunnar and Anna Claire came to his side.

"You ready?" Gunnar asked.

As he watched Mara sit down to eat, finally smiling at something the other females were saying, he heard his beast roar deep inside his mind. That woman was his mate, and he knew he'd do anything to keep her safe. It was already time to touch her to complete the mating, but it would have to wait a little longer.

"I'm more than ready." Luca's words were meant in two ways, and he had no problem admitting it to himself that he'd found the female that would be the love of his life.

Chapter 10

When they entered the town square, Gunnar drove around to the side of the building the sheriff had shown him on the map. As the angel had promised, the lights were out, and it was dark enough they shouldn't be seen entering the door.

Luca shifted his eyes, making the area easier to navigate as they stepped out of the car. The last time he'd been in that building was to have a private meeting with the sheriff after his brother had been killed. No one knew about that visit.

Ransom's death sent Luca into a spiral, and he'd begged the angel to give him information about his brother. Luca wanted to know if he made it to the other side peacefully. Garrett didn't want to get involved, because it wasn't his right to check on the dead. After a breakdown in the office, the angel blinked out, returning in a fraction of a moment.

"He's fine. He's going to be with your parents once he crosses the veil." The sheriff's words were comforting, but also like a punch to his chest. It didn't help him as much as he thought it would. At least Ransom was above with the gods that created their kind and not with the demons after what he'd done for his uncle when it came to finding Anna Claire.

"Focus," Gunner mumbled at his side. "We need the information the sheriff can get us to protect your mate."

All of the Morgan brothers had become his rock over the last two years, and they knew when he was unfocused, he was reliving the death of the one male in his life who was his constant.

"I want this information so Mara can live in peace," he replied, jutting his chin out toward the door where Garrett had just stepped out. "Let's get what we need and head back to the house. My beast is antsy without her."

The small walkway up to the door felt like it was miles long as his focus moved from his past to his future. Mara's natural scent was like a tattoo on his brain. She'd been aroused earlier when he drained his blood into a glass for her, and when he locked eyes with her, he saw a glimmer of hope there. She knew they were going to be tied together through his touch when it happened.

"I have already started the search, but I'm going to need Anna Claire to direct me to what she saw the last time." Garrett closed the door and locked the deadbolt. "There are no officers in the building. Only the dispatchers, but they are on the third floor. Please, come to my office."

The three of them stood behind the sheriff as he took a seat in his chair. Anna Claire stayed close to Gunnar, but leaned over slightly to point to certain tabs across the top of the page displayed on the screen.

"Click on the message boards tab," she instructed. "Now, scroll down alphabetically until you find something that might be associated with shifters or vampires."

Garrett did as he was told, and once he was on the board, she showed him the search bar.

"You're going to have to dig deep," she advised. "They use a lot of code words. The idiots who came to my clan two years ago were not as tight-lipped about their posts. I found it after a few simple searches, but I know I saw something about bloodsuckers in the search results."

"We have people who monitor the dark web, but I haven't had access to it until today. My detectives usually work these looking for anything in our county, but they focus on human trafficking and illegal drugs. No one has said anything about the shifters since they came out several years ago." Garrett cursed as he typed in word after word after word.

"Keep looking," Luca growled when Garrett leaned back in his chair. There was a lot of information on the shifters, but he still hadn't found anything on vampires. "Mara only feeds on shifters who donate their blood, and she doesn't know how many of her kind live among the humans."

Theresa Hissong

"Wait." Garrett had an idea, working his fingers across the keys, cursing when he came up with information on a coven of human feeding vampires in Northern California and New Orleans. "Damn. That's not what we need."

"I have a feeling Mara is a very rare kind of vampire," Gunnar pondered aloud.

"She's one of a kind," Luca replied softly. Gunnar laid his hand on Luca's shoulder.

"We will be home soon," he promised. "Then you can be with your mate."

As the sheriff navigated the dark web, Luca felt the tightness in his chest. Someone was after another person in his life that meant the world to him. He had so much faith in his brother's ability to protect himself, but it hadn't saved him.

Mara swore she would be stronger than any shifter if she fed regularly. If he mated her, fed her, and nurtured her, could she heal from a bullet to the heart? How did you kill a vampire, anyway? That was going to be their next conversation, and after that…he was going to mate her.

"Look here," Garrett ordered, interrupting Luca's thoughts. The angel pointed to a message board claiming a group of holy men had been on a rampage across the states to kill any type of vampire they could find.

The chat rooms were ablaze with information on shifter vampires, and one of them stuck out, claiming to have already been in contact with a young female…Mara.

Mating Scent

"They're already here," Luca bellowed, seeing his town's name...and *hers*. "They're coming for her, and she's too weak to protect herself. We need to get back to the land...NOW!"

The sheriff printed the messages off the dark web and handed them over as they fled the office, pushing Anna Claire into the truck. She sniffled in the back seat, still dealing with her own PTSD from being hunted a couple of years ago. This new threat was going to be as bad, if not worse, than when the other humans came for their clan two years ago.

Gunnar turned around in his seat as Luca floored the truck, trying to get back to the clan as soon as possible. As it was, the drive was twenty minutes, but he made it in fifteen. With the rate of speed he was doing coming down the long gravel drive, Drake and Rex were already on the porch with shotguns in hand. When they noticed it was Luca and Gunnar, they set the guns down, but by their golden eyes, Luca knew their beasts were right under their skin.

Luca's nature wasn't recessed either.

"Tell us," Drake barked as he met them at the truck.

"They know about Mara, and there are already hunters in the area. I need to speak with her," Luca said in a rush. He pushed past the Morgan brothers and marched into the main house. His eyes fell on her small body as she was fast asleep on the couch. Seeing her in respite calmed him enough to speak to her softly, bringing her out of her slumber. The last thing he wanted to do was scare her when she first woke up.

"Wake up, my little vamp," he hummed. "We need

to talk. Things are not good."

He wanted to give her a moment to let her brain awaken, but at the news of bad information, she jerked, sitting up and letting the blanket puddle in her lap. "Hunters are here, aren't they?"

"Yes," he admitted, nodding sadly. "I'm not going to lie to you. I'm worried. We all are."

"What do we need to do?" she asked, pulling the tie from her hair and regrouping the strands to make a less messy ponytail. It wasn't the time to notice how beautiful she was when her hair was mussed around her head, but he couldn't help it. Mara was his mate even if they hadn't touched yet. Anything she did would be beautiful to him.

"Come see what information we found," he advised. "The Morgan brothers like to gather at the kitchen table for meetings. It's more comfortable there."

The walk from the living room to the kitchen table caused the air around Luca to thicken. He knew it was his own mind panicking over the news and the things they'd found on the dark web concerning Mara.

He would be touching her tonight. There was no doubt about that. She needed the strength to protect herself, and from what he understood, his vein was going to be more sustenance for her than a cup of blood from his wrist.

"Luca, I'm scared," she whispered as they walked. "I fled from the coven, and I've been good at laying low since I came here. I don't understand why they want to kill me. I'm not a bad person."

"I know, honey." He crumbled, turning when they

reached the threshold of the main kitchen area. "My clan and I will always keep you safe."

"It's my nature to protect my shifter family," she cried. "That's what I was made to be."

Luca stared into her sapphire human eyes. He saw the tears as they welled up, and he wanted to kill the hunters for her, but he had a feeling she was going to be the one to save them when the hunters came the next time. Mara was a warrior, and he was going to make sure she was strong enough and knowledgeable enough to do just that.

"After this meeting, we will retire to my cabin, and we are going to make sure you and my clan have the protection we need."

"Okay," she agreed.

Gunnar laid out the printed sheets from the sheriff and organized them across the long table. "Mara, I need you to read these. If you see something that might be a lead as to who these people are, we need to know. Even if it's a small amount of information. Anything you can provide to us will help us keep our clan and you safe."

"Let me see what it says." Luca noticed her hands shaking as she picked up each piece of paper, setting it down before moving on to the next. She was halfway through before she froze, leaning in to read over the text again and again.

"Did you find something?" Luca asked.

"This, right here," she paled. "I know who this is."

"Tell me," Luca snarled, feeling his beast rush to the surface. He had to tighten his muscles to keep his bear from bursting through his skin.

"It was the delivery driver who brought food and restaurant supplies to the diner," Mara gasped once they showed her what they'd seen on the dark web. "It was a new guy, and I'd never seen him before. My senses were on fire. He creeped me out, but I found Gaia, and I had her finish the delivery."

"We need to get Gaia over here," Drake grumbled as he pulled his phone from his pocket.

"I'm sure she's asleep. It's late," Mara frowned.

"She will come," Luca assured her. "You'll understand soon."

"Understand what?" Mara looked confused, and he wanted to tell her, but it wasn't his place.

"Gaia will explain everything," he promised. "Please, trust me on this."

"I do trust you," she admitted.

Mara heard a car enter from the road, and so did the bears. All of the males pushed their chairs away from the table and stood as one. They moved as their bears did, slowly, but with grace, toward the front door.

Tires crunched along the gravel path leading to the front of the main house. Headlights dimmed, and Mara saw her boss behind the wheel, but there was something different about Gaia. She didn't look the same as she did when they were at the diner.

When her boss emerged from the car, she wore a flowing, white dress made of soft cotton. Her feet were adorned with sandals she'd never seen sold in any stores, and even though the night was a bit chilly, she didn't have a cover over her sleeveless arms.

As she approached, a shock caught in Mara's throat, and she sputtered at the sight. Gaia. Her eyes…they were…swirling.

"Gaia?" Mara gasped. "What's going on?"

"We should go back inside," Luca suggested, but Mara wasn't having it. It was obvious her boss wasn't quite human, and she wanted answers.

"What are you?" Mara asked when Gaia touched Drake's shoulder as if she was giving him comfort, and Tessa, the male's mate, didn't have anything to say…nor did she lash out at the female for touching her mate. Mara had never seen that before, and confusion racked her mind.

"Mara," Gaia sighed as she reached the top step on the porch. The female's eyes cleared and turned a beautiful shade of green. "Like Luca said…come inside. There are a lot of things you don't know about me. Things I've kept from you to keep you safe."

"You know what I am?" she angered.

"I do," Gaia nodded. The woman pushed past all of the clan and entered the main house ahead of them, walking directly into the kitchen and taking a seat to the left of the head seat at the table. It was almost like she knew her place in the clan.

"I need answers to a lot of questions," Mara said once they all gathered around the table.

"We will explain," Luca promised, and Mara felt his words. She trusted him with her life. Even though they'd only begun to chip away at the fact they were destined to be mates and she barely knew him, Mara would put her life in his hands. She knew he would be honest with her.

"Everyone sit," Drake encouraged, holding his hand out toward the empty chairs. Mara took the one next to Tessa where she could see Gaia.

"Someone please tell me what the hell is going on," Mara finally blurted once the table was full. Her fists hit the table and everyone turned when the sound and strength echoed throughout the room.

"Mara," Gaia sighed, reaching across the table to take her hands. "Let me show you what I am."

Mara hesitated but took her hand when Luca nodded, giving her his strength through his actions. The moment she touched her boss and the owner of the diner, a vision popped into her head.

The earth…empty and void of human, animal, and supernatural life. Creation. Trees growing in the vitamin-rich soil. Gods…the gods…playing with the perfect habitat. Dinosaurs…great fires from volcanos…ice and snow…destruction…and then…peace. Nothingness like the beginning.

A man, emerging from a cave, wearing the pelt of an animal to cover his body from the cold. More men and women…children…human.

More gods…playing with the humans, giving them the blood of a shifter…turning them into animals. Some of them did so of their own free will…others were ruled by the moon at its fullest phase. Wolves.

Mara gasped and jerked her hand away. "You? You are…Mother Earth? You created the world?"

Mating Scent

"Yes, dear, I created the planet. The gods created everything else and stole my home," Gaia replied.

"But...you're human?" Mara was confused, and rightly so.

"I have been here in my human form for many years," Gaia acknowledged. "I befriended Drake, Rex, and Gunnar's mother. We had a pact. If something happened to them, I would be the one to watch over them."

"So, you're their protector?" Mara pressed. As much as she was confused, the information she was being given started to make sense. "What about the sheriff?"

"He knows, and he is not of our kind," Gaia barked. There was obviously some bad tension between her and the sheriff. Mara had seen it when he came into the diner and they'd snuck off to her office. She'd heard some things, but it was mostly arguing about the bears.

"What is he?" Mara asked, crossing her arms when everyone narrowed their eyes. "If I'm going to be a part of this clan, I need to know everything."

"This is going to take a while." Luca took a protective stance behind her, and she could feel the warmth of his body. It surrounded her.

As they sat and talked, Mara was astounded at the information she was given. She had no idea that the sheriff of the town was an actual *angel*. Not only was he an angel, he had been put on the earth to care for the panther shifters who also inhabited the area.

The more information she learned, the sadder she became. All of the shifters around her were made by the gods, and she already knew that her kind were not. She was made from the flesh of the devil himself.

There was a balance between the gods and devil's games. She knew that, but her care for Luca could be a ruse. Were they destined by the gods or the devil? Was their possible mating predetermined?

"I need a moment to myself, please," she said, standing up so fast, her chair fell back from the force, but Luca was there to catch it before it hit the floor. Mara didn't even take the time to right it before storming out the back door. The only place she had to go was back to Luca's cabin, and that was her goal.

"Take your time, dear." Gaia's voice floated on the breeze as she stepped out into the night.

"Mara," Luca growled, using his own speed to gain on her. "Talk to me. Mara!"

His growling behind her brought her more comfort than she expected, and knowing he was on her tail made each step back to his cabin a bit more relaxing. The moment they both crossed through the threshold, she turned on him, baring her fangs.

"So, this is all fake," she barked, gesturing between them with her hand. "Me and you. It's a game? They did this, right?"

"Mara, no," he replied, shaking his head. She tried to ignore the sudden scent of his mating need, but the pheromones he was putting out into the air were too much to resist. "Our connection. It was written before we were ever born."

"I know how matings work, Luca," she scoffed, leaning toward him and holding her breath. She couldn't speak with his scent in her face. "But how could you love someone like me? I'm not even of your kind. I will most likely outlive you, too. The only way to kill me is to drive a stake through my heart or behead me."

"No one, and I mean *no one* will get close to you," he vowed, making a fist and putting it to his chest...right over his heart. "I already have fallen for you, Mara Wood. I don't give a fuck what you are, or who you are, or if you turn into a goddamn skunk. You are mine, and I am yours."

She heard his confession, and the part about the skunk made her chuckle. "A skunk? Really?"

"I'm being honest, Mara," he sobered. "I want you as my mate. My bear wants you as his mate, too. I am the only male who can protect you and accept your strength. It would be my honor to have you protect me with the proper feeding of my blood."

"You'd...you'd be willing to let me feed from you weekly? Sometimes more than that?" she cried, knowing what she was asking was a long shot. In one of her old clans, the males would only give her blood once every ten days, because they didn't want her stronger than them. Their egos wouldn't allow it. All they wanted was to use her body in exchange.

"Why are you so scared to mate me?" he guessed, narrowing his eyes. "There's more that you aren't telling me about your past, isn't there?"

How could he look into her eyes and see the pains of her pasts so easily? Would he think she was a whore? A desperate vampire who would do anything for a drop of blood?

"My past hasn't been the saintliest," she admitted

with a dark laugh.

"Tell me," he ordered.

"Let's sit," she offered, finding a spot on his couch. He sat at the other end, turning toward her. They didn't sit close enough to touch, but there were only a few inches between them. It was the closest he'd ever gotten to her, and she craved the moment they actually touched for the first time. "I will tell you about myself, but you need to listen. I didn't have the greatest start to my life as a vampire."

"I'm here," he promised, but his words meant more. Luca was offering his ear, and his heart was in it. She nodded and relaxed into the couch cushions.

"Ten years ago, I was out with my friends," she began, stopping to hold up her hand when he opened his mouth. Yes, she looked twenty-three and had *been* that age since she was turned. "I got separated, and in that time, I accidentally stumbled upon a group of men who had several women cornered in a bathroom. When I started to defend them, the males turned, and I saw their red eyes. Every horror movie I'd ever seen came rushing to my mind, and I knew they were vampires."

She paused for a moment to compose herself. What she had to say next was going to make Luca angry.

"After I was turned, my maker brought me into his coven. They lived with a bear clan in New York state. The males there would offer me sustenance, but for a price. They wanted my body, too. My maker brainwashed me into thinking that was what my life would be like."

Mating Scent

"Are you fucking kidding me?" Luca's bellow echoed throughout his cabin. She knew he wouldn't like her confession, but she continued. He needed to know everything.

"I was there, on and off, for eight years, Luca." She sighed, remembering her old life. "One night, I finally snapped. I saw the error of his ways, and after research from a few females in our coven, I knew I could suppress my vampire side if I just quit feeding. I'd still need blood, but I didn't need it as often."

"Not drinking blood makes you weak," he said with a frown. "Why would you do that to yourself?"

"It beat the alternative," she said, giving him a knowing look. That look sent his eyes into a change. The golden hue of his bear made an appearance, but she continued with her story. "I lost weight. A lot of weight. My coven leader noticed, and he forced me to feed off of a bear. It gave me enough strength to sneak into his room at the clan's home, driving a stake through his heart. I fled that night."

"Gods," he cursed.

"I ran, and eventually, came here," she admitted. "I found a job at the diner, and I thought I was in a shifter-free town until the panthers came in to eat. I knew I couldn't blow my cover by meeting and maybe hooking up with them, because they had an alpha, and the alpha knows all. Then the Morgan brothers came in, and I noticed they were friends with Gaia. I should've left town then, too, but I didn't. I'd suppressed my basic need for blood, finding a male who shipped pints on the black market. It was enough to keep me sated and strong enough to get out of bed each morning. Recently, that has changed. My five pints a month has dwindled down to two. I can't function on that little amount of shifter blood."

"You already know we are mates," he said softly, holding out his hand. "Touch me, and I will provide for you."

"Is it that easy?" she asked, scoffing at the end of her question.

"It hasn't been that easy for me," he replied. "You are only seeing part of the picture. My life hasn't been the best life. I turned on my own uncle because of the things he did to Anna Claire. Then, my brother was murdered by humans. He was my best friend. I've lived in misery for the last two years, and meeting you has given me a ray of hope."

"I knew about your brother, and I apologize for snooping," she admitted.

"Ransom was a good male…the best," Luca admitted. "I'll never forget him, and I hate that he suffered. That's what kills me the most."

"He's at peace now," she reminded him.

"I know," Luca said after taking a deep breath. "I know."

Chapter 11

There was no competition on the trauma they'd both had in their lives, but Luca knew he could make her whole again. His bear was even antsier to touch her, but his human side didn't think that night would be the night he touched her and made Mara his forever mate.

"It's for the best if you stay here tonight," he proposed. "You can stay in my room, and I'll take Ransom's bed."

"I wouldn't put you out," she denied. "I can sleep in the other room."

"No." He shook his head and refused to accept her offer. "Take my bed. I will sleep better knowing you are safe here."

Mara gauged his expression, and she finally caved

after a moment. "Okay, but let me at least make you breakfast in the morning. I don't have to work tomorrow."

"Deal," he smirked. "Do you need one of my shirts to sleep in?"

"I guess so," she said with a scowl, knowing she didn't have anything else to wear, and that made Luca's beast rumble with approval. She would be wearing his clothes. "I should've grabbed the bag from Anna Claire."

"Let me get you something," he mumbled and fled to his room to find the perfect shirt; long enough to cover the parts of her he was so tempted to reveal and soft enough to comfort her.

"Thank you," she said when he set the shirt on the back of the couch.

"There's a bathroom in the hallway," he advised. "First door on your left."

As she left the room, he felt the ache of her absence. The only thing keeping his feet planted firmly on the ground was knowing she wasn't far away.

"It's getting late," he announced as she returned. He swallowed hard and tried to keep his erection down. She looked like she belonged in his clothes.

Her long, brown hair fell over one shoulder, and the black shirt he'd chosen for her made the blue in her human eyes more pronounced. Her lips were perfect, and he wanted to know what she tasted like.

"I can scent you," she breathed, nothing more than a whisper. "Your mating scent is strong."

She was giving off a scent of her own, but it was desire. Her arousal hung in the air, and he took a step toward her out of a burning need to taste it on his tongue. "I want to touch you and make you mine."

"I'm starting to like that idea more and more each moment that passes, Luca," she admitted. "I know the spring mating season is hard for your species, and I also understand how you *know* who your mate is by the way your bear behaves and speaks to you."

"It was written in the stars that you were going to be mine," he reminded her as they both took a step toward each other. "Are you sure you want this?"

"Will you honor and protect me?" she asked, tossing out a vow. "Will you eventually love me with all of your heart and soul?"

There was no hesitation in his mind at her questions. "Love will come as time passes for us, but I already have this deep yearning to do as you asked. I want you at my side, protecting each other and *our* clan."

She hesitated for a moment, and her eyes glistened with unshed tears. Her hand trembled as it raised from her side. "Take my hand, Luca. Let nature handle the rest."

He didn't just take her hand. Luca wanted his lips on hers the moment the mating connection hit them, and that was exactly what he did. With his ability to move quickly, he took her hand and pulled the tiny female to his chest, pressing his lips to hers.

A short gasp broke through both of their lips when the magic of a mating struck them. For Luca, the connection slammed into him like a sledgehammer. Mara grabbed a handful of his shirt and kissed him harder. His snarls and her hisses sent him over the edge, scooping her up into his arms to take her to his bed.

"You know how this works, right?" His voice was deeper; his beast fighting to be right under Luca's human skin. The animal wanted the connection to his mate just as much. His bear would die for her…kill for her, and that was the way their kind had been made when the gods decided to play with their creations.

At least they got the mating for life part correct.

Mara pushed his shirt up, and because she was so much shorter than him, he took the material and ripped it over his head. Her lips landed on his pec right over his heart. "Mate me, Luca. This feeling…"

"I know, my little vamp," he growled as he slid his belt from his jeans, popping the first button. "I will mate you as my kind does, and I will mark you first. When you mark me, I need you to drink. You're going to need your strength for the next few days."

When their eyes met, hers were changing from the beautiful blue to a pink and red. She needed blood, and he was going to give her what she needed. Their fangs thickened in their mouths as they kissed again. He had no problem feeling their sharp points against his lips. It just made his cock harder with each pass over them with his tongue.

"On the bed," he ordered. She did the undressing of herself, and he was shocked to see she was completely bare under his shirt…no bra…no panties. "Gods, you are beautiful."

Mara was stunning. She might've been small, but she had shape to her body. Her breasts were perfect for

Mating Scent

him, and the rosy tips made his mouth water.

"I'm going to mount you from behind, but after we connect with our mating, I want to make love to you until the sun appears over the horizon tomorrow."

Luca had finally found something to live for…*someone* to live for, and as he ran his hand up his new mate's back to tangle his fingers in her hair for the mating, he realized that there was a reason why he was left on this earth.

Mara.

She gave him hope.

***

Mara had never found a male in all of the years she had lived with the old clan that made her feel the way Luca did just by looking at her with so much passion. Those men were a means to an end, and she knew it.

The touch of a shifter mate was magical, and she'd heard stories for years that it was an unbreakable bond. She wanted that, and she knew she was getting that with Luca the moment they touched for the first time.

"Mara," he moaned as his cock breached her body. The warm slide of his cock caused a shiver to roll through her body. Her fangs thickened in her mouth, and she knew her eyes were as red as they could be with the small amount of blood she'd had from him earlier. "So receptive for me."

"Oh, Luca," she hummed as he gathered her long hair in the palm of his hand, tightening his hold on her as per their mating rituals. "More, please."

His thrusts were harder, more intense, with each in and out movement. He guided her with his left hand firmly grasping her hip while the other hand prepared her for his bite.

"I am going to mark you," he snarled as he gathered her hair in his fist, pulling her back to his bare chest. There was no warning as he struck, and the feel of his canines in her neck caused her release to rush to the surface.

Mara cried out, begging for more of his cock. She felt him swell inside her, and when his seed released from his body, she bucked, knocking him to the side. Her eyes were fully red, and her fangs were thick in her mouth. There was a frenzy running through her immortal body.

"Drink from my vein as you mark me as your own," he offered.

The strike was desperate, and she relished his blood flowing into her mouth as she drank it down like a starved predator. The warm liquid was overpowering, and she felt her body accepting his offering.

Each muscle group in her body warmed, filling out as his life force flowed through her human body. The strength of her mate was now her own, and she would do everything in her power to protect him and his clan.

Chapter 12

Luca made love to her for the next two days, and she'd grown in size since he'd fed her a proper amount of blood. Where she'd once been skin and bones; a skeleton under a fine layer of flesh, her muscles had filled out, giving Mara the curves of a temptress. He'd never thought he would gain so much satisfaction from feeding his mate, but then again, he never knew that his life source would also be hers.

As he watched her sleep, he basked in the knowledge of what that meant. They were connected with an even tighter bond than just his animal nature. She had gone through her own mating ritual with the drinking of his blood during their mating night.

His fingers brushed over the spot on her neck where he'd marked her. It'd scarred over perfectly, and it was a sign that she was mated to a shifter. He carried the same mark on his own skin, and he would wear it proudly.

There would be times when she would not be with him, and he knew she would be able to protect herself with the renewed strength she had from his blood. The beast inside him grumbled at the thought of anyone laying a hand on her in harm, and he wanted to wake her up to tell her to quit her job at the diner. She should be at home with her new clan.

However, he would never force her to do that. She would make her decision to either live and work on the land with the Morgan clan, or she would keep her position with Gaia, and that thought did calm him a bit. Gaia would protect her, too.

"Luca?" Mara mumbled as her eyes fluttered. When she woke up a little more, a smile pulled at the corner of her lips. "Are you watching me sleep?"

"I am," he replied, pushing a strand of hair away from her face.

"What are we going to do today?" She stretched, tightening and releasing all of her renewed muscles. She hadn't been lying when she'd confided in him about her true nature and what drinking his blood would do for her.

"How about we gather your things from your little house?" he suggested. "I want you to live here with me."

Her brows pinched together as she thought about his statement. Mara gathered the sheet around her bare breasts and sat up in the bed, turning to face him. "I can do that, but I want to keep my job with Gaia. I love working there."

"I had a feeling you would say that," he admitted.

"Are you asking me to quit?"

"No," he promised with his hand over his heart. "I wouldn't ask that of you. I'm just trying to sort out our new life together. I know that matings are fast-paced, and some mates can be overwhelmed by it all. Especially if they are not a shifter."

"Luca, I know how matings work," she reminded him. "Things will be awkward as we learn and grow, and while I would love to stay here all day, there is no reason for me to sit around and wait for you to come home from the fields. I can still do my own job, and it does have its benefits. I will be home every night when you arrive after your work is done for the day."

"You are quite independent, aren't you?"

"Well, I've had to be." Mara shrugged, but her face fell. "My parents were dead, and I was out on my own. I had to fight for the things I had and hard work was how I made ends meet. It wasn't long after my twenty-third birthday that things changed for me." She flashed her fangs, recessing them after she'd made her point.

"What happened when you woke up a vampire? I'd like to know the details if you are willing to tell me." Luca wanted to know everything about her, and since she'd been turned by a vampire, he wanted to know that information, too. She'd spoken of how she'd killed him, but that was the extent of it.

"I woke up after being taken to a home in New York state. When I gathered my senses, I was like this and there were people surrounding me. They smelled so good, and it wasn't until one of the males cut his wrist that I knew what I was craving. I cried when I drank his blood. They had to pull me away so I wouldn't drain him. Each of the…what I know now as shifters, cut their veins for my first feeding. Being a new vampire meant I needed a lot of blood. I couldn't deny the urgency and need to feed then."

"Who turned you?" Luca demanded.

"His name was Bruce Decker," she admitted. "He was the coven leader for the area, and he lived alongside a very willing bear clan. He'd brainwashed them into being our food in exchange for sex."

"So, you're actually thirty-one?" Luca asked, knowing she still appeared to be in her early twenties.

"I don't age…none of us did." Her admission didn't take long for his brain to catch up on the math. His focus redirected back to her youthful face when he felt her palm gently touch his cheek. "I will outlive you, Luca, and that's something we need to discuss."

"That's not going to be a topic today, Mara," he denied with a slash of his hand. "We have plenty of time." He knew that was a lie. He'd seen how quickly a life could be taken.

Mara smiled sadly, but pulled his face toward hers. "Okay, my new mate, what's on the agenda for today?"

He welcomed the distraction and took her lips in a heated kiss, only releasing her once he'd had his fill. "Today, I want to formally introduce you as my mate to my clan."

"Let me shower, and I'll be ready to go in twenty minutes."

Mating Scent

"I'll help you," he offered, reaching for the sheet covering her new body from him.

It took them another few hours to leave the house, and by that time, Ada had already made lunch for the clan. The Morgan brothers were taking a day off from their work in the fields, because it'd rained earlier that morning, and since everything was planted, they just needed to let Gaia do her work with the weather to make the crops thrive over the summer.

"Everyone, I know you've all met Mara Wood, but I'd like to formally introduce her as my mate," Luca announced once everyone had gathered in the kitchen. Saying it out loud made what they'd done fill his heart with a joy he hadn't had in a very long time.

The females doted on her, and they passed her around with hugs and whispered words of support. The brothers slapped him on the back and congratulated him the way male bears usually did when one of their clan found their mates.

"We will celebrate tonight with a huge meal," Rex bellowed and held up a beer he'd pulled from the fridge right as Luca and Mara came through the back door. Drake passed Luca a beer and gave him an approving nod.

The family he'd been adopted into was everything he'd ever wanted…he and his brother wanted. The elders were thriving, and Ada and Anna Claire were wonderful mothers. He sensed the pregnancies in them both and Drake's mate, Tessa. It was mating season, and he wasn't surprised there would be a new round of cubs born in the winter when they all settled down for their hibernation.

As he watched Mara, he wondered if she could carry his cub. It was a joy to the males to have their own cubs, but with Mara being a vampire, he wasn't quite certain what that would mean for them.

"Everything okay?" Gunnar asked as he bumped his shoulder against Luca to get his attention.

"Wonderful," Luca replied with the right amount of enthusiasm to keep the male from digging with his questions.

Gaia propped open the back door to the diner as the driver unloaded the produce from the back of his truck. It was the same male who'd come the week before, and she was certain it was the male who was a part of the human faction who wanted all vampires dead.

She had a plan, and if it worked, there would be one less piece of shit roaming the area to kill Mara and others like her. As much as she hated the gods, she also hated the scummy humans who used their god's name for a reason to murder the innocent...no matter their species.

"Oh, damn," she feigned. "I have to write you a check this week. Could you come to my office?"

"Sure," he replied, but he looked past her like he was looking for Mara, and that was exactly what Gaia wanted for the human male. She needed him distracted.

She sensed her bears waiting in the office. They would ambush the human male and serve out shifter justice on one of them after they interrogated him on his plans for Mara.

"This place is empty today," he noted as they made their way down the hall. "Where's your cook and that beautiful waitress?"

"She's off today, and I closed the store for the breakfast crowd," Gaia admitted, and she was being honest. "I want to get my annual cleaning done since it's the middle of the week."

"Good plan," he grumbled under his breath. She could feel the male's agitation, and she was sure the brothers could scent his deceit a mile away. This male was looking for Mara, and she wasn't sure if he had plans to grab her if she'd been the one to answer the door.

"Hand me the invoice," she ordered, holding out her hand. When he released the paper, she used her free hand to open the office door. "Come inside. We need to chat, anyway."

Gaia stepped back as the male came face to face with two very angry grizzly bears in their partially shifted form. Two deathly growls echoed through her tiny office as Drake reached for the human, but the kidnapper was faster.

"Gun!" she yelled as he drew a weapon from his side.

Gaia's human body was pushed to the ground the second the first shot rang out. When she realized that Drake had chosen to save her and not attack the male who was running for the back door, she dug down deep in her body, feeling the vibrations of her own anger.

Rex went after the male, ducking when another shot rang out, but Gaia was already building a wall of vines across the back door of her diner. She heard the human male curse, Rex growl, and her vines being ripped from their purchase on the back door.

"Drake, go!" Gaia pushed him away and gained her footing, following the head of the clan toward the male. When they turned the corner, a smirk lifted the corner of her mouth.

The human male was suspended in vines, his hands turning white from the lack of blood to his extremities. His face was turning red, and his eyes were bugging out of his head. The problem with it was that he wouldn't be able to speak. So, Gaia waved her hand, pulling back the vines from taking the male's life.

"Who are you, and why are you after the female?" Drake demanded, making her vines useless because he wrapped his large hand around the human's throat. "You have a choice here. If you give me the information I need, I will let you live…for an extra few minutes to pray to the god you worship. You can ask him for his forgiveness before I send you to meet him."

"Fuck you," the male spat. "You'll rot in hell like the female abomination."

"Wrong answer," Drake snarled, releasing his bear's claws. Blood began to trickle from the small puncture wounds at the man's neck. "You have one more chance. Tell me what your plans are for the vampire female."

Rex stepped to his brother's side. He kept his shifted hands at his side, but Gaia saw him flex each

Mating Scent

finger as it shifted. They may have just become Mara's family, but the female was going to be protected because she loved Luca, and Luca loved her. No one would hurt the female as long as the Morgan clan had a breath in their bodies.

"She's an abomination, and our organization is responsible for wiping them off the face of the earth." The man spit and sputtered his words. A thin stream of blood trailed from his nostril when Drake slammed his head against the back door.

"Who else is looking for her? How many of you are here?" Rex calmed himself enough to allow Drake to ask the questions.

When the male began to squirm, Gaia waved her hand again, adding more vines to the male's legs…and she might've just made them a little extra tight around his manly area, too. When he let out a high-pitched squeak, she smirked again. She'd have to remember that if the sheriff pissed her off.

"There are only three of us left," he admitted, his voice still an octave higher than before the vines. Maybe she should geld him before Drake takes his miserable life.

"What do you mean by three left?" Rex chimed in.

"The other vampires killed the last two guys, and I'm guessing you are going to make my team one less hunter after today."

"Where are the other two men?" Drake pressed, still holding the human's throat. When he didn't answer, Drake slammed his head into the door again and tightened the hold on his throat. "If you want to breathe, you will answer my questions. If you lie, I can scent it. If you hesitate in your answer, I will not release my hold. So, let me ask you again. Where are the other two men?"

"Memphis," the male choked, and Drake released his hold just slightly so the man could draw in a deep breath. "In a rental off Shelby Drive, and they're waiting for more hunters to arrive from the West Coast."

"Address," Rex barked as he fished his phone from his pocket.

When the human rambled off the address, Rex entered it into his phone and nodded once he locked in their location. "Okay, you can kill him now. We have a place to drop his body as a warning."

"What?" the male cried out. "I gave you the information. Why are you going to kill me? Come on man. I…" Drake used his powerful hands to snap the male's neck, leaving deep gashes as a calling card that a shifter had taken the human's life and not a vampire.

"Gaia," Rex spoke softly, but she was getting angrier by the second. This faction of humans were killing vampires all over the world. Some of those vampires were just like Mara…innocents. They didn't ask to be turned, nor did they want to live off of human or shifter blood.

"This is so messed up," Gaia sniffled. "No one should be hunted. Especially those like my sweet Mara. She doesn't deserve to live in fear."

"Gaia," Rex said her name again. "Gaia, release his body so we can get this done. The quicker we eliminate the problem, the sooner we can all live in peace."

Mating Scent

"What peace, Rex?" she barked, waving her hand to make the vines disappear. When the male's lifeless body fell to the ground, Drake took it out back to the delivery van. "Will you ever have a time when the humans aren't trying to kill you?"

"That's something we will always have to live with, but since we are known to them now, it'd be best if we start locking down the compound. I've been working on a security plan, and now that the cubs are getting older and new ones are being born, we will have to work on preparing the land to be enclosed."

"You're making yourselves prisoners," she reminded him.

"I know the panthers have a very solid security system," Rex began, holding his hand up when Gaia started to say she would help. "I'd like to hire them to help us fortify the compound."

"I think I agree with you, brother," Drake admitted, casting a glance over his shoulder. "The bodies will start piling up if we don't do something to protect our families."

"Whatever you build, I will gladly add my touch to the perimeter." Gaia would add thorny vines to the outer facing fencing to keep anyone from climbing it to access the Morgan clan's land. She'd do whatever it took to make sure her family was safe, too. She owed that much to their mother.

She owed that female her life.

Chapter 13

Mara *paced the tiny living* room at Luca's cabin. She felt something crawling under her skin. Part of it was the need to feed and strengthen herself. It would have to wait. Luca was working in the fields, and the last thing she wanted to do was to be around the clan when she was feeling…off.

It wasn't just the need to feed. Mara felt something ominous on the horizon, and she knew it had to do with the hunters. Her worry didn't ease when news had come that Drake and Rex found the delivery driver and forced information from him before dumping his body on the steps of a house the hunters were using in Memphis just twenty miles from the clan's land and a short eight miles from the diner.

They'd been that close the entire time, planning and

preparing to kidnap her. She'd heard of other vampires being captured when she was at her old coven, and the information that was shared about the outcome of that would put fear in the hardest of vampires.

They weren't easy on their captives. The human males who hunted her kind under the guise of religion were also some very sickening men.

Mara shook her head to jar the memories of the things she'd been told all those years ago. She would never tell Luca, or any of the Morgan clan, that information. It was too disgusting to repeat. Drake's murder of the delivery driver gave Mara a bit of satisfaction. The demonic side of her hoped the human male was scared as he took his last breath.

She spent the afternoon napping, making an excuse of being tired when Tessa had messaged her phone asking if she wanted to have lunch with the mates. By four in the afternoon, Mara knew she wouldn't be going anywhere for the night. The last time she'd fed off of Luca was too many days ago, and the blood was quickly leaving her body.

Her hand slid across her stomach, and she winced at feeling the indentation just under her ribs. When Luca came home, he was surely going to notice her weight loss, and she needed to talk to him about her hunger. It was more imperative now that she keep up her strength. He knew she needed blood to be strong, but she didn't want to impose on him since they'd recently mated.

How was she going to tell him to feed her frequently? On a schedule at that? He had been very concerned with her need for blood, but they were still learning each other as a couple. Mara knew the importance of open communication.

By the time she heard his truck pull up to the house, her fangs were thick in her mouth, and she could hear his heartbeat as he walked through the door. She sat as still as possible in the recliner facing him when he stepped over the threshold, and he could tell something was wrong.

"I stopped by your house and picked up your mail," he began, but paused, dropping his belongings by the door. "Mara? What's wrong? Look at me?"

"I can't," she slurred around her fangs. "I'm starving, and my body is going into a frenzy from hunger."

"Oh, my little vamp," he sighed, rushing to her side. The moment he dropped to his knees at her feet, she struck. Tears poured from her eyes as his quick intake of breath hissed through his teeth. She wrapped her arms around his shoulders, squeezing him tight as the blood filled her mouth. It was warm and tasted like everything she needed to survive, and it wasn't a simple instinct. She needed him more than she ever thought she'd need a male.

"Drink your fill," he whispered, taking his large hand and cupping the side of her face. Mara cried harder as he used his thumb to wipe away the tears that flowed from her eyes. "Why did you let it go this long?"

He knew she couldn't answer, but she tried anyway. Her mumbled words around his wound were not heard, but she did apologize. The need to drink was just too much.

"Take what you need. Shhh, my love. There is no

reason for you to talk right now," he cooed. "I need you strong for what's coming, and if you need more, I can give you that."

She swallowed again, finally feeling a bit of relief, but she jerked back when he began to sway.

"Oh, my gods, Luca," she gasped, grabbing him by the material of his light jacket to hold him upright. Her strength allowed her to pull his body up enough to sit him on the couch next to her. "I'm so sorry. I didn't mean to take that much."

"It's fine, Mara," he promised, reaching over to clean the rest of the tears from her face. "My body will regenerate what you drank. Give me a few minutes."

"I've made you too weak," she cried, helping him wipe away fresh tears from her blood red eyes. "I shouldn't have waited so long."

"No, you shouldn't have," he scolded.

"I'm sorry," she repeated. "Here, let me care for you. Lay your head in my lap."

Mara urged him to lay his head across her, and she ran her fingers through his long, dark hair. He closed his eyes for a moment, absorbing her touch. His bear must've liked it because there was a faint purr-like sound coming from his chest.

"You know," she whispered as she continued to stroke his hair. "I've never seen your bear."

"That's right," he smiled, finally. "I haven't shifted in months. Not since we came out of hibernation. I think I can remedy that tonight if you'd like?"

"As long as the two of you are up for it," she answered, knowing he needed to shift to heal anyway. "I can make you dinner first. Then, if it's safe enough, maybe we could go for a walk in the woods."

"It's not safe, but we can at least get out closer to the house. We should be fine to hang out in the backyard over by the garden."

"I'd like that," she replied, leaning down to kiss his forehead. "Let me get you a pillow. I want you to rest while I make a plate for the both of us."

On his nod, she made sure her mate was comfortable before going to his kitchen where she'd set up the slow cooker earlier that morning to make a meal of roast and veggies for their dinner. When she returned, he was already asleep.

"Luca, I need you to eat something," she said, waking him up with a full plate of food in her hand. "I'm sorry I took too much."

"It's fine, Mara," he promised and sat up on the couch. He frowned when he looked over at the things he'd dropped by the door. "You received a package today, and I'm assuming it's a donated blood bag from another bear. I could scent it all the way home. It's probably for the best if you stop having those sent to your home. I don't like it."

Oops. She'd forgotten about her shipments. It was the first of the month, and her guy was always on time, even if he didn't send enough to satisfy her cravings each time.

"I won't drink it unless you are too weak to feed me," she admitted, but the deep growl coming from her mate had Mara backtracking in her words. "What if you are hurt? I would need blood to protect you and our clan."

"You just called the clan ours," he smiled. "I like that, a lot."

"I'm serious, Luca," she huffed, taking a bite of potato off of her own plate. "I think it's best if we keep some extra stock on hand given the current threat to me."

"The only stock you'll be keeping on hand is my own blood," he corrected. "At no time would I ever be okay with you drinking another shifter's blood."

"Again, I am serious, Luca," she repeated. "I know we've talked about my kind, but I don't think you totally understand how powerful I am when I have been fed properly."

"I do, actually," he admitted, finishing off his meal before he set the plate on the side table. "I have no idea how you were made for a shifter, but I get the mythology better than you think. We were all once scary stories to keep children in line. Your kind makes sense though. I know you are a rare type of vampire, and I've been trying to find others like you who live with shifters to understand how you benefit them. You, at your best, could be a fighter…a Guardian like the panthers have…to our clan. It's in my nature to protect my mate, but the more I learn, the more I am accepting of the fact that you could protect us. We need you on our side."

"There are no sides, Luca," she admitted. "Our mating was beautiful, and I have feelings for you. Your clan is becoming a part of me…family."

"Could you say that you are starting to fall in love with me, Mara Wood?" he smirked, but it wasn't cocky. His smile was that of happiness, and she responded

Mating Scent

with her own.

"Luca O'Kelly, I have feelings for you that go well beyond simple infatuation," she admitted, but laughed when he lunged for her. He was obviously feeling much better since she'd taken so much of his blood.

"You love me," he chuckled. "Admit it, Mara."

She didn't even have to think about it. He'd shown her so much respect since she'd told him exactly what she was, and even she knew how their animals ruled their matings. There was no doubt in her mind that Luca was going to be her forever.

"Luca, I do," she sniffled, trying to hold back the tears of joy at finally admitting to him, and herself, the feelings she carried for him. "I do love you."

"And I you," he said right before his lips crashed down on hers.

"Are you strong enough?" she worried.

"I am fine," he promised as he ran his finger down the V of her shirt, pulling it away from her skin so he could use his tongue to trace her cleavage. "My body has strengthened, and all I want to do is make love to my mate."

"I…" she panted as he pushed aside her bra to lap at her hardened nipple. "I agree."

"Good thing I am off tomorrow," he chuckled as he reached for her jeans. "I'm not letting you leave *our* bed for at least twenty-four hours."

Luca lost count of how many times he'd made love to

Mara. They'd spent the better part of the night before and most of the morning in bed.

He loved seeing her desire as she climaxed for him, and he was prideful when it came to learning how to satisfy her body.

"Are you going to come for me again?" he urged, slowing his thrusts as she begged for more. His thumb rotated around her clit, building her release. She wanted his cock to move faster, but it was so much sweeter when he held her off.

"You've got to give me more," she gritted with her fangs bared.

"Are you hungry, my little vamp?" he chuckled, never losing his rhythm. "You look weak."

He was teasing, but he knew their romp was taking a lot of her energy. Although she'd drank way more than her fill the night before, his shifter nature regenerated his blood within a few minutes afterward. He would give her everything he had if it kept her strong enough to protect herself when the other humans came for them.

He wouldn't think of the information the Morgan brothers gave him when they'd dropped the dead human male at the house the others had used for their headquarters. Drake and Rex searched the home for the other males, but came up empty. That meant they were still on the loose.

Luca didn't want that for his mate, and he sure as fuck didn't want them coming to their clan to find his mate. He would do anything in his power to keep her strong, because he understood the importance of having her as a warrior who could protect the clan and

Mating Scent

the cubs that would be born in the coming winter.

"Feed, Mara," he ordered, giving her his neck. "I need you to be strong."

"Luca," she hummed as her release was close.

"I want to fuck you senseless while you feed from my vein, my little vamp," he admitted. "Take my vein...now!"

The moment she struck, so did her orgasm. He relished in her bite and focused on his mate's release, giving her everything she needed to live and be strong. He bled his life's force into her mouth while showing her how deep his love had grown for her over the weeks since he'd realized they were to be fated mates for the rest of their lives.

The moment her fangs broke free from his mating mark, he found his own release, falling to the side from exhaustion. But his little vamp wasn't done, climbing on top of him as her hands wrapped around his cock, bringing it back to life when she wanted to continue their lovemaking.

Mara's body thickened and her muscles grew even stronger from his blood, and her body's curves were more amplified as his blood gave her strength.

"I love seeing you like this," he said, using both of his hands to trace the curves of her enhanced body. "I'll always want you like this."

"I'm thick when I'm fed," she giggled.

"I like you thick and full of my blood," he smirked, pulling her down so he could capture her lips.

His eyes fell on her mating mark as she rode his cock. She wasn't the only one who liked to bite. His canines thickened in his mouth as he salivated with the thought of marking her again. She must've sensed his need and pulled her hair to the side, giving him her neck. She climaxed the moment he struck.

Luca would never tire of their lovemaking, and he rolled her to her back when he lapped over her mark. It gave him much satisfaction to see the two red marks where her shoulder and neck met. It told other shifters she was his, and he would keep the scar red and swollen every single time he was buried deep in her body.

They both cursed when his phone rang somewhere in the living room. The last thing he wanted to do was to slide free from his mate's body, but she urged him to go because it might be important.

And her safety was on the line. His choice of making love to her was thwarted by a call from the sheriff.

"Do you know why the Memphis P.D. found a dead body at a rental home tonight?" Garrett's voice was unusually deep. The lawman was an ally for the shifters, but when it came to humans, he was adamant about keeping the two species separate unless he was involved to stop shifter law from being on the nightly news.

"One of three, and possibly a lot more, Garrett," Luca barked into the phone. "I'm not sure what you want to know beyond that."

Luca didn't want to talk about the murder over the phone. His time spent with Drake Morgan had him a little paranoid about putting their information out into the world, and thankfully, the sheriff understood his coded speech.

"They are conducting an investigation into a murder." The sheriff paused for a moment after taking a deep breath. "It's not my jurisdiction, Luca, but the murder was close enough to the state line for us to be worried."

"I have no idea what you're talking about, sheriff," he hedged. "If you'd like to take a break from work tomorrow morning, we do have a bushel of early vegetables you can pick up on your way into the office."

Yes, Luca was talking in code, and the angel knew it.

"When will you be here?" he snarled, feeling his heart break all over again, knowing the angel.

"Seven minutes," Garrett replied. "And be ready. The information I have is not good, Luca."

His first thought after he tossed the phone was to grab Mara and force her to dress. "We may have a war tonight. I need you to be at your best. Feed from me one more time."

"No!" she barked. "I've had enough from you already."

His anger got the best of him, and he felt his beast pushing at his skin. "God damn it, Mara! Listen to me. You are probably about to see my bear for the first time, and knowing that these hunters have information on my brother just makes me feral. Feed, damn it! I don't want to worry about you should the next hour turn into a war."

She stared into his eyes as she pulled on her jeans. She was still undressed from the waist up, and he had to focus on what was to come and not the beauty of his mate's body.

"Do it!" he barked, pulling his hair to the side. "Feed on me!"

She struck and gulped down mouthfuls of his blood. When she pulled back, her face was painted red. The blood was flowing from his vein, and she stopped before it weakened him too much. He started to argue, but her appearance and a raised hand stopped him.

"I'm full," she admitted, looking at her arms. With her half-naked body exposed, he saw her muscles forming…growing…thickening. "Let me close your wound."

He nodded and let her use her tongue and saliva to stop the bleeding. "How strong are you right now?"

"Stronger than I've ever been," she admitted. Her body was twice as big as he'd ever seen her. The color of her face was no longer stark white. With his blood pumping through her body, she was at her best, and when she flexed her newfound muscles, he relaxed enough to head for the door when he heard the sheriff's car turn into the driveway.

"I'll call the brothers," she offered. "I'll have them meet you and the sheriff outside."

"Thank you," he calmed, pulling her to his side. "I love you more than you know, and I want you strong so you can protect yourself."

"At this point, Luca…I'm strong enough to protect the entire clan."

Chapter 14

"*The two other human males* are looking for Mara tonight," Garrett announced the moment he stepped on Luca's porch. The angel didn't wait to be invited in. He just marched right past Luca and headed straight for Mara. "They're starting at the diner. I have officers there watching the place."

"Have you called Gaia?" Mara was worried about her boss and the protector of the Morgan clan. She shouldn't be involved in this mess, and Mara knew she had to do something to keep the hunters from hurting her new family.

But how? What could she do to get them away from Gaia and the clan?

"Gaia is on her way here," he admitted, looking at his watch. "She should be here in less than five minutes.

I've warned the Morgan brothers, too. They are taking precautions with their mates and cubs. We will meet them at their house once you're ready."

Mara was more than ready. She didn't want anyone knowing what she was or where she was staying. Being a rare vampire should've kept her secret hidden a lot better, but after hearing of the things they'd found on the dark web, she was quickly realizing that most secrets weren't really secret anymore. Someone somewhere always knew of things they shouldn't, and from her time with the coven, she knew how to handle those who threatened her existence.

"When they come for me, I will handle them," she announced, feeling the last taste of Luca's blood strengthen her body.

"No," Luca barked, slashing his hand through the air. "I will not let anyone near you."

"You don't have a say in this, Luca." When was he going to learn that she was stronger than him and his entire clan combined? She'd already shown him a taste of her strength with just a cup of his blood. Now that she'd been fed properly, she could fight an army.

"I trust Mara's abilities," Garett interrupted, but paused when Luca spun on him. "Look, now is not the time to get protective. Everyone needs to play a role in this, and Mara knows what she's doing."

"How do you know so much about me?" she blurted. The angel never seemed fazed about what she was, and she wondered how.

"I know a lot about too many things, Ms. Wood," he stated, glancing toward the door. "Gaia is here. We need

Mating Scent

to go."

The three of them set out for the main house, seeing the three brothers already standing on the small back porch. Each one of them held a shotgun in their hands.

"The mates are secure," Drake advised as he stepped aside for Mara to enter the house right as Gaia rushed through the front door.

Mara met her in the living room as the two females hugged and Gaia whispered, "I know you can stop this, and I'm on your side. Do what you need to do, and I will make sure hellfire falls upon anyone who comes close to this land."

"Thank you for believing in me," Mara returned the soft whisper, praying the males didn't hear their short conversation.

The women stepped back from each other, right as a shot rang out, shattering the window in the front door. The men lunged for them, but Mara spun out of the way. Drake took Gaia to the ground and the scent of human blood filled the air.

"Gaia, no!" Mara cried out when she saw blood on her boss's back. They'd struck her. "Fuck."

"Get her out of here!" Drake barked as he scooped Gaia up into his arms, running for a hallway off the kitchen. There was a commotion at a door. Drake was beating on it until someone opened it. The noise was cut off for a moment, but the next bullet coming through the house stopped their worry and put the clan on high alert.

Luca lunged for her, but the strength she had was more than he realized. With her enhanced speed, she zipped out of the living room, out the back door, and was close to the road within a second. There were several cars lining the road maybe a half-mile down. She scanned the area and saw the human males gathering. One of them had a bow and arrow. He lit the end of it, and her heart stopped when a bright orange, white, and blue flame erupted from its tip.

It was launched half a second before she bared her fangs and ran as fast as her vampire legs would move her, knocking the son of a bitch on the ground with a missing throat. Human blood dripped from her chin as her eyes flared red.

When she spun around to attack, the next one to plan an attack on her clan was preparing another arrow as she scented the first one starting to burn the house.

Yes...*her* clan! The Morgan clan was her family, and she would stop at nothing to keep them safe.

Twenty men circled her, pointing weapons of various sorts at her heart. She froze for a moment, and gasped when she scented her mate and the other males coming in their various forms. Two were in their human form. Two were bears, roaring and snarling in the male's direction.

A flash of white light stopped them, and in its place stood Garrett, but he wasn't himself. His body was larger, angrier. His eyes were as white as snow and his face was glowing.

"Stop now!" the angel barked.

"Never," one of the younger men replied as he shot his weapon. The bullet hit her shoulder, but she immediately knew it was nothing more than a regular bullet. It wasn't even made of wood.

Idiots!

Mara's nature took over, and as she hissed in his direction, she used her thumb and forefinger to dig into the hole, pulling the bullet from her flesh. She looked at the male, cocked her head, and flicked the bullet with her bloody fingers. The bullet flew through the air, faster than it'd ejected from the gun, striking the male between his eyes, dropping him on the ground as his human life fled from his shell of a body.

"I am stronger than all of you," she hollered. "I will take you down one by one."

She scented fear from most of them, but she didn't have time to attack before her mate, Luca, in his bear form, lunged for one of them, biting the male in the shoulder and taking his mangled body to the ground.

She realized the other bear was Gunner, since Drake and Rex were in human form with their own weapons. Gunner followed her mate's lead and began the attack.

And that was when the bullets started flying, and in that moment, a storm of all storms hit the area. Wind and hail followed a downpour of rain. She knew it was Gaia, sending water from the sky to extinguish the fire in the main house. The man with the bow and arrow was trying to light his next flaming attack, but the water was too much for his fuel.

She couldn't worry about Gaia or the females inside the main house as they protected their cubs and their pregnant bodies. It was a distraction she couldn't let inside her mind. Not being focused could get everyone killed.

The human hunters scattered. Some of them got into their cars and the other ones fled on foot. The bears looped off into the woods around the clan's land, and Mara went for the cars just as her mate's bear turned to look for her at the forest edge.

She wasn't going to worry for him, because she knew he was strong enough to handle the men on foot. With his blood in her body, she jumped from her standing position and landed in front of an old SUV, using her strength to slam her hand into the hood, stopping the speeding vehicle as if it was nothing more than a child's toy. The sudden impact sent the human male through the windshield, and she watched as his body slid across the pavement several feet past her. When she turned to find more hunters, she could hear his heartbeat slowing. He was dying, but she wasn't going to let him die without seeing her vampire face as he took his last breath.

It didn't take more than a second or two for her to kneel on his chest, capturing his throat with her hand. His eyes flew open with what was left of his will to live. She bared her fangs and went for his throat, ripping his head from his body. The fear she saw in his eyes and scented from his body was enough to spur her on to chase the second truck that was now almost a mile from its original location.

Inside, there were three males, and she did the same as she'd done to the last, stopping them with her strength. Her hand shot out, slamming into the hood, denting it…disabling it as it came to a sudden stop. One male wasn't wearing a seatbelt like the first one in the SUV, and his body came out very similar to the one before. She didn't even look at his mangled body because she heard his heart stop as he was launched through the air.

Her focus was on the other two who were bleeding and trying their hardest to unbuckle so they could run. She wasn't going to let them get away.

Not on her watch.

She heard roars and gunshots behind her, feeling her heart ache at the fight she wasn't there to help with in defending her new home, but the human men in that truck couldn't get away. Their deaths were quick, and she left them to bleed out on the street as she rushed back to the land to see the bears and the brothers in their human forms, bleeding from various wounds and gunshots.

More headlights. Two sets this time. At least five more hunters came onto the scene, shooting their weapons as their feet hit the pavement. They wasted no time in jumping into a fight they were going to lose.

Her body trembled from the anger she felt. It'd been a long time since her vampire nature was strong enough to feed off her emotions. With that knowledge, her eyes glowed red, and she felt her body swell. Even when a bullet hit her thigh, she didn't even flinch. Her blood leaked from the wound, but it wasn't life-threatening.

No, she would heal, and it sure as fuck wasn't going to slow her down. As it was, she'd killed four human hunters, the clan had taken out another five. That left eleven of those worthless beings for her to take on as her brothers and mate were forcing their animals to shift and reshift to heal themselves.

A roar unlike anything she'd ever produced from her body echoed off of the trees and budding branches of the spring seasonal growth. Several of the humans froze, fear freezing their faces in a shocked pose like pausing a horror flick.

Her vampire side relished in seeing it on their faces, and she attacked, using her speed to hit four of them in a matter of seconds. She stumbled once as a bullet entered her hip, and she went to her knee when one took out her shin. They were trying to pierce her heart, but she kept her left shoulder tucked, not allowing them a direct target to take her out.

If they got a shot off to her head, it wouldn't kill her. Only decapitating her would do the trick, but she refused to go down that easily. However, as the blood leaked from each wound, she felt herself weakening. She needed to feed, and none of her enemies would do.

Luca's bear roared from her side as his bear tried to climb to his feet. There was a lull in the attack, and Mara rushed to his side, biting into her wrist. "Drink my blood. It will speed up your healing. I don't have enough strength to fight them all. I'm going to need you."

The beast tried to pull away, but she was still stronger than he was at the moment, and Mara pushed her bleeding wrist to the bear's teeth and grabbed his snout, closing his mouth around her arm. She felt his bear lap at her wrist several times before she had to move. The humans were regrouping and reloading their weapons.

Mating Scent

She needed blood, and she was either going to have to kill them quickly or find a bear to feed from that wasn't her mate. Luca was too weak, even with their blood exchange to help her. Drake and Rex were hurt, and Gunner wasn't in much better shape.

The winds were still causing chaos around them, and a flash of white light was her only hope. Garrett couldn't kill humans because of his status, and she wasn't going to ask why until after their fight was over. He did do everything in his power to take the human's attention off the bears while they recovered. It would take some time for them to be strong enough to help her kill the remaining hunters, but time was fading quickly.

Branches fell from a tree between the hunters and her clan. Gaia was controlling the weather around the land to help them fight, but Mara knew she wasn't going to have the power to finish this battle.

"Mara!" a female voice called out. When she recognized Tessa's voice, Drake was already trying to gain his footing to protect his mate.

"Tessa! No!" he hollered. The leader of the clan was angry, and his body shifted, shredding its human skin and tearing his clothes. He tried to run for her, but he stumbled, faltering in his attempt to protect her.

"What are you doing?" Mara yelled as she used her speed to reach Tessa as she ran down the yard, using various trees for cover. "You can't be out here!"

"The fuck I can't," the female snarled. "You need blood, and only the females can provide for you. You need your strength."

They both ducked behind a huge oak tree as a

hunter shot toward them, narrowly missing Mara's head. She grabbed the pregnant female and pulled her to her knees. "This is stupid, Tessa! Drake is going to be so angry."

"I don't care," she growled, her eyes glowing with the presence of her bear. The female took her long, blonde hair and pulled it to the side, exposing her neck. "Feed from me. I promise I will go back to the house as soon as you have enough blood to strengthen. You are our only hope."

They both looked around at the male bears who were injured and shifting to try to repair their bodies, but the hunters were gathering for another attack. It wasn't right for Tessa to risk herself and their unborn cub to feed Mara, but she understood the female's intentions. It brought a tear to her eye as she spotted the pulsing vein on Tessa's neck.

"Thank you," Mara whispered as she struck. The blood of a shifter was her life source, and since she was feeding from a female, it wouldn't hurt her because she was mated. Tessa was the best choice for her to get blood from, and knowing she could feed and take her own renewed blood to her mate, she drank her fill, closing the wound on Tessa's neck once she had enough.

"Now, get out of here!" Mara's words were harsh, but Tessa touched her cheek before taking off for the house. Mara's body strengthened enough to clasp her hand around the female's arm and give her a boost of speed to get her to the front door of the Morgan home. Once Tessa was safely inside with Gaia, Mara turned for the hunters, and as her eyes glowed a deeper red, so did her desire to end this fight…once and for all.

Luca shifted again, taking on his bear form. He didn't know that his mate's blood would boost his healing, but he was certainly glad it did the first time she'd offered her vein. Tessa was watching him as Mara fed from her neck. Drake's mate gave him a soft smile as Mara's head tilted back from her strike to the vein, and she gave Luca a knowing nod. He wouldn't think of how much trouble she would be in once Drake healed, but he would thank her and hopefully calm the leader's anger at his mate putting herself and their unborn cub in danger to help Mara win this fight with the hunters.

His mate moved too fast to track as she returned from getting Tessa to the house. He jerked back when he blinked and she was there with her bleeding wrist at his bear's mouth again. "Luca, I need your help. You have to take more of my blood. We have to finish this together."

He couldn't speak in his bear form, but his beast did what she'd asked, knowing the vampire was his mate and his equal in protecting his clan. Her blood worked its way through his body at a fast rate, powering him. When she looked into his bear's golden eyes, the beast huffed in a sign he was ready. They both turned toward the hunters and that was when things turned worse.

Or better, if you were a vampire hell-bent on saving your family.

Luca lunged for the first hunter who rushed them, taking the male down easily. Fucking humans were so frail. Didn't they know how stupid their plans were when it came to fighting the paranormal?

With his mate's renewed strength, she broke the necks of three more males in a matter of seconds. There were only a few left, and those men were smart…and armed. The bullets wouldn't kill him or his clan unless they were struck in the head or heart. He knew Mara could withstand more, but at what cost? A bullet to the heart of any species would kill them.

His bear roared when she was struck again. This time, the hunter who used the truck's door as a shield got off a round that hit his mate in the forearm. She dropped to her knees and used the hand on her uninjured arm to grab at her arm that was bleeding. He didn't realize what she was doing until he heard the faint sound of the spent round hitting the ground. She'd dug the bullet out of her arm and laughed maniacally when the wound healed on its own.

The male screeched when she zipped to his side, wrenching the rifle from his hands and grasping him around the neck. There were no words for him before she squeezed him so tightly, his eyes swelled in their sockets. The pressure from her hold stopped the blood flowing to his brain, and right before he lost consciousness, she yanked her hand to the right, removing his head from his body. It was brutal and bloody, but something in his mate's renewed eyes told him she really was a force to be reckoned with when she was using her full nature on an enemy.

Mating Scent

Drake, Rex, and Gunnar had finally repaired their bears and rejoined the fight, taking out several of the humans who finally gave up and tried to flee the area. They'd come to kill Mara, and his clan wasn't going to let them off where they could regroup and return to attack another day.

Mara assisted Drake in killing one male who'd hidden under the remaining truck. Gaia's wind storm confused them, and the mother of all creations on the earth was detailed enough that she kept the bears and Mara from being hit or bothered by the storm. The humans, on the other hand, became confused, lost in a sea of debris. It gave them the advantage they needed to end it for good.

The moment Mara took the last hunter's life, the wind stopped and the sky cleared over the clan's land. A flash of white brightened the area for a second before Gaia and Garrett were there to check on everyone. Garrett's first order of business was to toss Luca and the others some clothes, and Luca watched as the sheriff checked on Mara.

"I'm good," Mara panted, taking a calming breath. She sat heavily on her ass and leaned against a tree by the end of the driveway. "Fucking hell. That was intense."

"Intense?" Luca questioned, trying to calm his beast he'd just recessed into his mind after forcing the animal to give him back his human body. "That was…"

"Speechless?" Gunnar snickered.

"Well, yeah," Drake, breaking his usual quiet and calm nature, laughed. "Your mate is a warrior, Luca."

"That she is," Luca agreed. And like their ancestors passed down from generation to generation, he dropped to one knee at his mate's feet and pressed his fist to his heart as he bowed his head. "You are the love of my existence and a warrior to my clan. Mara Woods, you amaze me, and I would trust you to fight for my family any damn day."

"I don't think your ancestors put it quite like that," she chuckled and started to reach for him, but froze when Drake, Rex, and Gunnar all followed him in their stance.

"We can't express our gratitude for the things you did here tonight to keep our clan safe," Rex stated, mimicking Luca's pose.

"I agree," Gunnar choked, pressing his fist to the ground after removing it from in front of his heart. "I am forever in your debt. Whatever you want, it is yours."

"I'll take a homecooked meal," she teased, reaching for Luca. "You guys don't have to do this. I know it's part of your nature and history, but this is the twenty-first century. Females are warriors, too."

"No," Drake finally spoke up, lifting his eyes from the ground. Luca was a bit confused. Drake was the strongest of the Morgan clan, and he was always seen as the strength of the clan. He'd never seen the male show much emotion, but when the eldest male looked at Mara, there were tears in his eyes. "Mara Wood…you took an offering from my mate, and then…then you cared for her and got her to safety when I…when I couldn't. I will never be able to express how much that means to me. You saved us. You saved my mate and cubs. You will forever be my kin…my sister, and I will honor you until I take my last breath."

Luca and the others were frozen as Drake did something Luca had only heard of. He closed his eyes and bared his canines, biting into his hand…not his wrist. Once the blood pooled in his palm, he made a fist and squeezed, dropping blood at Mara's feet.

It was a sign of respect. In fact, it was a rare sign of respect only reserved for warriors of the grizzly race who'd done unspeakable tasks to protect a clan. Mostly, it was used when the savior of a clan was killed in battle after giving their life to protect an entire bloodline.

Mara gasped and Rex and Gunner chanted an ancient song softly while Gaia and Garrett watched quietly from several yards away. Luca had only heard of this from his father when he was just a cub, but he'd never witnessed anything like it in his lifetime.

His mate, Mara, had just been shown the highest respect in a clan that could ever be received.

"We honor you," Drake choked out as a tear fell from his eye. The grumpy bear was moved by Luca's mate and the things she'd done to protect them.

Mara must've known how their species honored warriors, because she followed Drake by biting into her palm and repeating what he'd done, dripping her blood over his as it mixed into the ground of the Morgan's land, blending both of their species on what was now considered hallowed ground. It was now marked as a sacred place, and by shifter law, no one, human or otherwise, would be able to desecrate it for the rest of time.

Luca lunged for her when the Morgan brothers raised from their knees. The ceremony was done.

"I love you," he bellowed. "You…you are amazing."

"I did what I had to do to save my family…my clan," she said, taking his lips as the clan cheered.

Chapter 15

Mara set a *cup of coffee* in front of her mate. He'd started coming to the diner every morning for breakfast after the final harvest was done and the weather was changing. It was almost time for his clan to go into hibernation for the winter months.

She still wasn't sure what she was going to do. Gaia promised her it would be okay for a three-month vacation so she could spend it with Luca, and Luca had no problem with whatever she decided.

The mates were getting closer to their due dates, and Mara knew they would all most likely deliver around the same time in December. She'd been studying up on caregiving for new mates, and if she were being honest, she'd prefer to be there for them instead.

It was no secret she was unable to have children, and as much as she wanted to give Luca a cub, they both accepted the fact that dream wasn't in the cards for them. They had the cubs of their clan family to love and protect.

"What has your mind working so hard?" Luca asked as she set his plate down. Her mate's hand captured hers and brought it to his lips, placing a kiss on her knuckles.

"Thinking about the mates and this winter," she admitted with a sad voice.

"You know I love you and I want whatever you want, right?"

"I do." Mara's smile was genuine. "I think I'm going to stay at the clan over your hibernation. It would bring me great pleasure to help the mates with anything they may need when their cubs are born. I have a feeling it's going to be hectic around there with three births."

"I agree," he chuckled. "This is the first year they all are with young at the same time."

"I know the males do most of the work in delivering their young, but I could always be a nurse if they need it."

"Are you still researching it?" Her mate was the most understanding male she'd ever met, and he loved her for whatever she mentioned she wanted to do or learn.

It took almost ten years for Mara to be happy and thrive in her vampire life, and if it wasn't for Luca, she would probably still be a shell of the woman she once was.

Mating Scent

"Yes," she agreed with a nod. "I am."

"I'm sure they will generously accept any help you'd offer," he replied and picked up his fork. "We are finishing up our prep for the winter, and I'm sure everyone will be glad once the fence and security system is finally finished."

"When does the Shaw pride think they will be finished?"

The panthers were hired by the Morgan clan to secure their land, putting up a fence around the perimeter and installing a state-of-the-art security system. It made Drake a little less grumpy knowing there was another line of defense to keeping their clan safe.

"Winter mentioned next week, but they've been working from sun up to sun down the past few days. I'm guessing it'll be done before the end of this week."

"They have been a great help to the clan," she agreed.

"I know you are strong, and I know you won't hibernate with me, but it gives me a little peace, too." Mara wasn't going to fuss at him for being so worried about her. It was endearing, and she would forever love him for his care.

"I'm going to hibernate with you as much as I can," she reminded him. "When I am not with you, I will care for the land and keep an eye on the new monitor room the panther's built beside the office."

"You are my hero, Mara," he advised with a sexy wink. "When do you think you can come home for the day?"

"I think she can head home now," Gaia interrupted as she came around the breakfast bar by the register. "Today is going to be a slow one, anyway. You two get out of here and enjoy your time together."

"Thanks, Gaia," Luca said as he crumbled his napkin and dropped it on his plate. "I'm going to take my mate home."

"Let me get my things," Mara chuckled as the bell over the door sounded and the sheriff entered with his head held high.

"Luca, Mara," Garrett acknowledged, turning his eyes toward Mara's boss. "Good morning, Gaia."

There was something in his eyes that told Mara their relationship might be more than what she thought. The angel appeared a bit smitten…maybe? Whatever that was, she was sure Gaia would work it out.

An angel and the creator of the natural world?

Odd, but okay.

"Get your things," Luca said, touching her lower back right before he leaned down to whisper in her ear. "I'm still starved. It's time I take you home."

His flirting would never get old.

"What brings you in today, sheriff?" Gaia asked, handing him a menu she knew he didn't need. The male came into the diner so often, she was sure he had it memorized.

"Thought I'd treat myself to a breakfast," he said with a shrug, but she scented something coming from his body, and it wasn't a man-made cologne. She didn't know if angels had a mating scent or even if they could mate.

"What's the occasion?"

"Peace, Gaia," he sighed in relief. "We finally have peace in the area, and I'm celebrating it."

Peace for Garrett was a blessing, and she was thankful her bears were finally happy and safe. She'd fulfilled her promise to the best friend she'd had for so many years once coming to this tiny community to find her own peace.

A sadness washed over her. She wasn't ready to return to the planet she'd created. It was almost like a punch to her gut when she realized she wasn't needed there anymore, and as she looked around the diner, the memories flooded through her mind.

"What's wrong?" Garrett blurted, going on alert.

"Nothing, sheriff," she whispered, holding back tears. "My thoughts are elsewhere and on a promise I gave to a long-lost friend. It seems I've completed that task, and I've made a great place here. The realization that I might need to return to my old home has me wishing I didn't have to go quite yet."

"What do you mean, go?" he bellowed, startling a mother who was sitting at a table close by.

"Shh, Garrett," she scolded. "This is not the place, nor the time to discuss my intentions."

"I disagree." The male gritted his teeth and stood. "I need to speak with you in your office."

"Fine," she sighed, and it wasn't out of frustration, either. Gaia was tired.

It was probably for the best if she started her plans for her departure. As she followed the sheriff to her office, she made a quick calculation of her belongings in her human form. She would give the diner to Mara and Luca. She trusted the vampire to continue her legacy and care for the place.

The brothers had finally found their happiness, and she'd done everything she could to protect them while they found their way in life and became fathers and mates. Her tiny house, she would put in one of their names. Maybe Mara would find another female like herself who was running from evil and needed a place to hide. Her little cabin on the lake would make for the perfect retreat. She'd make sure her place was cloaked enough to protect a female in need.

The moment they entered the office, she yelped when Garrett slammed the door and threw the lock, grabbing her gently by the arm. One second, she was staring at the tile floor while lost in her plans, and the next thing she knew, she was pinned against the office wall…

And the sheriff's lips were on hers.

"Garrett!" she gasped around his fiery kiss.

Epilogue

Many years later…

Luca couldn't explain how happy the second part of his life had been since he'd mated Mara. They'd gotten over the fact that she would never have his children, but that was okay. After the last twelve years of their mating, they'd found that loving their nieces and nephews from the Morgan brothers was enough to fulfill them. Yes, they weren't blood-related, but clan family was the same as if they'd been born as brothers and sisters.

Drake's son, Ransom Chance, or RC as he was called, and his brothers and sisters were thriving alongside their cousins from Rex and Gunnar's line. RC and their firstborn, Aria, had taken to learning how to run their own clan, following the lead of their father. The other siblings and cousins were learning the ways of being a shifter.

The Morgan brothers had brought several children into the clan over the years, and with each birth, their numbers grew and the bond of the clan was stronger.

The elders were lost over five years ago, Martha and Doug died within six months of each other, and Peggy and Alfred died the following spring. They were so close, and so well bonded, that once their mates died, there was nothing left for them. It was sad, and a little scary.

Luca knew Mara would outlive him since she was immortal, but she'd expressed many times that she would follow him in death just as the elders had done with theirs. It was unspoken, but he knew she would do anything to not live past him. It scared him that she would go to such great measures to make sure they were reconnected in the afterlife, but he finally accepted it. She would never tell him her plans, and for the foreseeable future, he didn't want to know. He was more focused on their time together while they were still alive.

The world had changed so much over the past fifteen years. Shifters were considered citizens of the world, and no one even blinked an eye when it came to their species. There was peace, for now, and Luca would take it. There were a lot of the humans who thought they were experts on their kind, but as with all shifter business, they kept most of their secrets to themselves. The news reports could speculate all they wanted, but the shifters were tight-lipped about their truths.

The humans, vampires, and other species of the shifter world lived in peace, and that was all he wanted. That was all they ever wanted. Yes, there were still bad shifters out there…just like there were bad humans, and if they came for his clan, they were ready. With the cubs aging toward their maturity, the clan would be even stronger. They would be thriving, and continue to thrive, adding generations to their numbers.

RC had taken to learning all he could about the other species, and even his father, Drake, had found an almost friendship with the panthers. There wasn't any animosity toward others as there was years ago. The old grumpy bear was finally accepting of the help the other shifters in the area were offering, and that made everyone in the clan happy for the connections. His son was very interested in the organization the panthers had established over the years, and much to Drake's chagrin, his son had aligned himself with Talon's daughter, Ember Shaw, to learn their strategies.

"What has you so lost in thought?" Mara asked as she cast her line again in the pond he'd had made on the clan's land five years ago. His mate liked to fish, and he was more than happy to make her a place she could find peace when she needed it.

"Thinking of the past and our future." He shrugged and watched as something bit at his bait, bobbing the line while the fish tested the tasty treat he'd attached to the hook in the water.

"Our future looks very bright," she reminded him.

"The sheriff and Gaia are working together to make sure no ill falls upon us anymore."

"They are," he agreed with a nod. His mate and Gaia had become even closer, and Mara still worked at the diner to that day. She would never leave Gaia, and from their close friendship, he knew Gaia would do anything to protect his mate. She considered Mara as family.

Even though his mate wouldn't need saving.

She was the strongest member of the clan. It took her attack on the humans all those years ago for Luca to realize that she was correct in her words. He'd be lying if he said he didn't question her when she'd originally said, with his blood, she would be stronger than the entire clan. Her words were true, and since she was a rare species of vampire, she'd aligned herself with the Morgan clan, vowing to protect them from anything that might befall them.

She'd, thankfully, not had to defend them since that night so long ago. The memories from that attack would forever haunt him, because he'd been unable to be her hero. But…he was male enough to accept that she was, in fact, the heroine of the story.

His mate was the strongest being on the planet, and he, and his clan, had promised to make sure she was protected and hidden, because if someone found out about her strength, they might come for her. They'd want to harness her abilities.

None of them would let that happen.

"Got him!" Mara laughed, giggling as the fish took her bait. She didn't use her inhuman strength to reel in the line once she hooked her catch. Luca had learned that she enjoyed the fight when they were fishing. She had something she enjoyed that reminded her of her human life, and he wasn't ever going to stop her from having the little moments where she could just be herself.

"Look, Luca! It's a beast!" Mara was grinning from ear to ear at her catch. The fish was easily five or six pounds, and he congratulated her as he watched his mate unhook it and gently release it back into the water. "We will let him go on to make new little fishes. The big ones have lived in this pond since it was created. They are the alphas."

They both laughed at her joke, but something brewed inside him. The moment she set her rod on the ground, he captured her face and pressed his lips to hers.

"You know I love you more than my own life, right?" he stated, becoming serious.

"Oh, my dear Luca," she breathed and hummed when he kissed her again. "I love you more than my own life, too. I cherish you more than the sun in the sky and the air in my lungs. You are the blood in my veins, and without you, I am nothing."

"No, Mara," he whispered, pressing their foreheads together. "You are everything…everything."

The End…

And they all lived happily ever after.

Other Books by Theresa Hissong:

Fatal Cross Live!
Fatal Desires
Fatal Temptations
Fatal Seduction
Fatal Intentions

Rise of the Pride:
Talon
Winter
Savage
The Birth of an Alpha
Ranger
Kye
The Healer
Dane
Booth
Noah
Taze
Storm

Morgan Clan Bears
Mating Season
Mating Instinct

The Ward Wolf Pack Novella Series
His Lost Mate
His Stubborn Mate
Her Protective Mate

Incubus Tamed
Thirst

Standalone Novella
Something Wicked

Book for Charity
Fully Loaded

Club Phoenix
The Huntress

Cycle of Sin on Tour
Rocked (A Rockstar Reverse Harem Novel)

About Theresa Hissong:

Theresa is a mother of two and the wife of a retired Air Force Master Sergeant. After seventeen years traveling the country, moving from base to base, the family has settled their roots back in Theresa's home town of Olive Branch, MS, where she enjoys her time with family and old friends.

After almost three years of managing a retail bookstore, Theresa has gone behind the scenes to write romantic stories with flare. She enjoys spending her afternoons daydreaming of the perfect love affair and takes those ideas to paper.

Look for other exciting reads…coming very soon!